THE BIG RANGE

Also by Jack Schaefer

THE BIG RANGE

JACK SCHAEFER

University of New Mexico Press | Albuquerque

22 21 20 19 18 17   1 2 3 4 5 6

Library of Congress Cataloging-in-Publication Data

Names: Schaefer, Jack, 1907–1991, author.
Title: The big range / Jack Schaefer.
Description: University of New Mexico Press edition. |
Albuquerque : University of New Mexico Press, 2017.
Identifiers: LCCN 2016052206| ISBN 9780826358455 (softcover : acid-free paper) |
ISBN 9780826358462 (electronic)
Subjects: | BISAC: FICTION / Westerns. | FICTION / Short Stories
(single author). | GSAFD: Western stories.
Classification: LCC PS3537.C223 A6 2017c | DDC 813/.54—dc23
LC record available at https://lccn.loc.gov/2016052206

Cover illustration: *Against the Sunset*, 1906. Frederic Remington (1861–1909).
Oil on canvas
Designed by Lila Sanchez
Composed in Adobe Jenson Pro 11/15

Contents

Author's Note

I like to write about the wide open spaces when they were still open and their wideness could enter into the people, some of the people, who left life's footprints on them. . . .

Back in 1940, after fifteen years of research and study, Harold E. Briggs published his *Frontiers of The Northwest*. A careful scholar, a competent craftsman, an uncompromising historian. A sound, thorough, authoritative book. As Dr. Briggs approached the end of the writing, some of the wideness of the land and the people and the historical movement he was chronicling entered into him. "The true story of western settlement," he wrote, "is best told when the broken lives it exacted are recorded, when romanticism and realism run hand-in-hand through the narrative."

Here are seven tales about seven people in which romanticism and realism run hand-in-hand. They tell of lives broken and they tell too of lives made whole by resolute acts of will, whether in the long living or the brief dying. They are primarily stories of character, attempts to depict the raw material of human individuality through action and plot. Each was based, in germinal beginning, on an actual incident of recorded fact. The background details were derived from my own study of the diaries and journals of the Western frontier. The cast is various: rancher, sheepherder, homesteader, town settler, soldier, miner, cowboy. Yet the essential purpose is the same throughout: to establish a distinct and individual major character and pit him against a specific human problem and show how he rose to meet it. And all of them, the characters and the stories that evolve from them, are conditioned by the wide-open spaces of the old West, in which the energies and capabilities of men and women, for good or for evil, were unleashed on an individual basis as they had rarely been before or elsewhere in human history. The four stories of the first section are grouped together because they are all first-person narratives told by the same narrator. I note now what I did not when I was writing these stories, that this narrator, John, has a habit of taking over the telling when the tale is grim, edging towards tragic. The three stories of the second section stand each alone in the sense that each is told from a separate viewpoint, one by a first-person narrator within the story and two by impersonal outside onlookers in the traditional fiction form.

It is little Miley Bennett taking care of his talking sheep in the Big Horn country who supplies the title and the underlying theme of this book. "It's big, ain't it? Makes a man feel big too." I would like to expand that theme here but realize that my stories must do that for me.

Jack Schaefer

Santa Fe

PART ONE

Jeremy Rodock

Jeremy Rodock was a hanging man when it came to horse thieves. He hanged them quick and efficient, and told what law there was about it afterwards. He was a big man in a many ways and not just in shadow-making size. People knew him. He had a big ranch—a horse ranch—about the biggest in the Territory, and he loved horses, and no one, not even a one of his own hands— and they were careful picked—could match him at breaking and gentling his big geldings for any kind of road work. Tall they were, those horses, and rawboned, out of Western mares by some hackney stallions he'd had brought from the East, and after you'd been working with cowponies they'd set you back on your heels when you first saw them. But they were stout in harness with a fast, swinging trot that could take the miles and a heavy coach better than anything else on hooves. He was proud of those horses, and he had a right to be. I know. I was one of his hands for a time. I was with him once when he hanged a pair of rustlers. And I was with him the one time he didn't.

That was a long ways back. I was young then with a stretch in my legs, about topping twenty, and Jeremy Rodock was already an old man. Maybe not so old, maybe just about into his fifties, but he seemed old to me—old the way a pine gets when it's through growing, standing tall and straight and spreading strong, but with the graying grimness around the edges that show's it's settling to the long last stand against the winds and the storms. I remember I was surprised to find he could still outwork any of his men and be up before them in the morning. He was tough fiber clear through, and he took me on because I had a feeling for horses and they'd handle for me without much fuss, and that was what he wanted. "You'll earn your pay," he said, "and not act your age more than you can help, and if your sap breaks out in sass, I'll slap you against a gatepost and larrup the hide off your back." And he would, and I knew it. And he taught me plenty about horses and men, and I worked for him the way I've never worked for another man.

That was the kind of work I liked. We always paired for it, and Rodock was letting me side him. The same men, working as a team, always handled the same horses from the time they were brought in off the range until they were ready and delivered. They were plenty wild at first, four- and five-year-olds with free-roaming strong in their legs, not having had any experience with men and ropes from the time they were foaled except for the few days they were halter-broke and bangtailed as coming two-year-olds. They had their growth and life was running in them, and it was a pleasure working with them.

Rudock's system was quick and thorough; you could tell a Rodock horse by the way he'd stand when you wanted him to stand and give all he had when you wanted him to move, and respond to the reins like he knew what you wanted almost before you were certain yourself. We didn't do much with saddle stock except as needed for our personal use. Rodock horses were stage horses. That's what they were bred and broke for. They were all right for riding, maybe better than all right if you could stick their paces, because they sure could cover ground, but they were best for stage work.

We'd rope a horse out of the corral and take him into a square stall and tie a hind leg up to his belly so he couldn't even try to kick without falling flat, and then start to get acquainted. We'd talk to him till he was used to voices, and slap him and push him around till he knew we weren't going to hurt him. Then we'd throw old harness on him and yank it off and throw it on again, and keep at this till he'd stand without flicking an inch of hide no matter how hard the harness hit. We'd take him out and let the leg down and lead him around with the old harness flapping till that wouldn't mean any more to him than a breeze blowing. We'd fit him with reins and one man would walk in front with the lead-rope and the other behind holding the reins and ease him into knowing what they meant. And all the time we'd speak sharp when he acted up and speak soft and give him a piece of carrot or a fistful of corn when he behaved right.

Hitching was a different proposition. No horse that'll work for you because he wants to, and not just because he's beat into it, takes kindly to hitching. He's bound to throw his weight about the first time or two and seem to forget a lot he's learned. We'd take our horse and match him with a well-broke trainer, and harness the two of them with good leather to a stout wagon. We'd have half-hobbles on his front feet fastened to the spliced ends of a rope that ran up through a ring on the underside of his girth and through another ring on the wagon tongue and up to the driving seat. Then the two of us would get on the seat and I'd hold the rope and Rodock'd take the reins. The moment we'd start to move, the trainer heaving into the traces, things would begin to happen. The new horse would be mighty surprised. He'd likely start rearing or plunging. I'd pull on the rope and his front legs would come out from under him and down he'd go on his nose. After trying that a few times, he'd learn he wasn't getting anywhere and begin to steady and remember some of the things he'd learned before. He'd find he had to step along when the wagon moved, and after a while he'd find that stepping was smoothest and easiest if he did his share of the pulling. Whenever he'd misbehave or wouldn't stop when he should, I'd yank on the rope and his nose would hit the soft dirt. It was surprising how quick he'd learn to put his weight into the harness and pay attention to the boss riding behind him. Sometimes, in a matter of three weeks, we'd have one ready to take his place in a four-horse pull of the old coach we had for practice runs. That would be a good horse.

Well, we were readying twenty-some teams for a new stage line when this happened. Maybe it wouldn't have happened, not the way it did, if one of the horses hadn't sprung a tendon and we needed a replacement. I don't blame myself for it, and I don't think Rodock did either, even though the leg went bad when I pulled the horse down on his nose. He was something of a hollow-head anyway, and wasn't learning as he should and had kept on trying to smash loose every time the wagon moved.

As I say, this horse pulled a tendon, not bad, but enough to mean a limp, and Rodock wouldn't send a limping horse along even to a man he might otherwise be willing to trim on a close deal. Shoo him out on the range, he told me, and let time and rest and our good grass put him in shape for another try next year. "And saddle my bay," he said, "and take any horse you'd care to sit, son. We'll ramble out to the lower basin and bring in another and maybe a spare in case something else happens."

That was why we were riding out a little before noon on a hot day, leaving the others busy about the buildings, just the two of us loafing along towards the first of the series of small natural valleys on Rodock's range where he kept the geldings and young studs. We were almost there, riding the ridge, when he stopped and swung in the saddle towards me. "Let's make a day of it, son. Let's mosey on to the next basin and have a look-see at the mares there and this year's crop of foals. I like to see the little critters run."

That's what I mean. If we hadn't been out already, he never would have taken time to go there. We'd checked the mares a few weeks before and tallied the foals and seen that everything was all right. If that horse hadn't gone lame, it might have been weeks, maybe months, before any of us would have gone up that way again.

We moseyed on, not pushing our horses because we'd be using them hard on the way back, cutting out a couple of geldings and hustling them home. We came over the last rise and looked down into that second small valley, and there wasn't a single thing in sight. Where there ought to have been better than forty mares and their foals, there wasn't a moving object, only the grass shading to deeper green down the slope to the trees along the stream and fading out again up the other side of the valley.

Jeremy Rodock sat still in his saddle. "I didn't think anyone would have the nerve," he said, quiet and slow. He put his horse into a trot around the edge of the valley, leaning over and looking at the ground, and I followed. He stopped at the head of the valley where it narrowed and the stream came through, and he dismounted and went over the ground carefully. He came back to his horse and leaned his chest against the saddle, looking over it and up at me.

"Here's where they were driven out," he said, still quiet and slow. "At least three men. Their horses were shod. Not more than a few days ago. A couple of weeks and there wouldn't have been any trail left to follow." He looked over his saddle and studied me. "You've been with me long enough, son," he said, "for me to know what you can do with horses. But I don't know what you can do with that gun you're carrying. I wish I'd brought one of the older men. You better head back and give the word. I'm following this trail."

"Mister Rodock," I said, "I wish you wouldn't make so many remarks about my age. One thing a man can't help is his age. But anywhere you and that bay can go, me and this roan can follow. And as for this gun I'm carrying, I can hit anything with it you can and maybe a few things you'd miss."

He looked at me over his saddle and his eyebrows twitched a little upwards.

"Careful, son," he said. "That comes close to being sass." His jawline tightened, and he had that old-pine look, gray and grim and enduring. "You'll have hard riding," he said, and swung into his saddle and put his horse into a steady trot along the trail, and that was all he said for the next four-five hours.

Hard riding it was. Trotting gets to a man even if he's used to being on a horse. It's a jolting pace, and after a time your muscles grow plain tired of easing the jolts and the callouses on your rump warm up and remind you they're there. But trotting is the way to make time if you really intend to travel. Some people think the best way is to keep to a steady lope. That works on the back of your neck after a while and takes too much out of the horse after the first couple of hours. Others like to run the horse, then give him a breather, then run him again, and keep that up. You take it all out of him the first day doing that. Trotting is the best way. A good horse can trot along steady, his shoulders and legs relaxed and his hooves slapping down almost by their own weight, do it hour after hour and cover his fifty-to-sixty miles with no more than a nice even sweat and be ready to do the same the next day and the next after that, and a lot longer than any man riding him can hope to take it

Rodock was trotting, and his long-legged bay was swinging out the miles, and far as I could tell the old man was made of iron and didn't even know he was taking a beating. I knew I was, and that roan I'd picked because he looked like a cowpony I'd had once, was working with his shorter legs to hold the pace, and I was shifting my weight from one side to the other about every fifteen minutes so I'd bum only half of my rump at a time.

It was a dark night when Rodock stopped by water and swung down and hobbled his horse and unsaddled, and I did the same.

"Might miss the trail in the dark," he said. "Anyways, they're moving slow on account of the colts. I figure we've gained at least a day on them already. Maybe more. Better get some sleep. We'll be travelling with the first light." He settled down with his saddle for a pillow and I did the same, and after a few minutes his voice drifted out of the darkness. "You came along right well, son. Do the same tomorrow and I'll shut up about your age."

Next thing I knew he was shaking me awake and the advance glow of the sun was climbing the sky, and he was squatting beside me with a hatful of berries from the bushes near the water. I ate my share and we saddled and started on, and after I shook the stiffness I felt fresh and almost chipper. The trail was snaking in wide curves south-west, following the low places, but rising, as the whole country was, gradually up through the foothills towards the first tier of mountains.

About regular breakfast time, when the sun was a couple of hours over the horizon behind us, Rodock waved to me to come alongside close.

"None of this makes sense," he said, without slacking pace.

"A queer kind of rustling run-off. Mares and foals. I've tangled with a lot of thievery in my time, but all of it was with stock that could be moved fast and disposed of quick. Can't do that with mares and sucking colts. How do you figure it, son?"

I studied that awhile. "Mister Rodock," I said, "there's only one advantage I see. Colts that young haven't felt a branding iron yet. Get away with them and you can slap on any brand you want."

"You're ageing fast, son," he said. "That's a right good thought. But these foals couldn't be weaned for three months yet. Say two months if you were the kind could be mean and not worry about getting them started right. What good would they be, even with your brand on them, still nursing mares that have got my J-tailed-R brand?"

"I'd be mighty embarrassed," I said, "every time anybody had a look at a one of them. Guess I'd have to keep them out of sight till they could be weaned."

"For two–three months, son?" he said. "You'd ride herd on them two–three months to keep them from heading back to their home range? Or coop them some place where you'd have to feed them? And be worrying all the time that maybe Jeremy Rodock would jump you with a hanging rope in his hand?"

"No," I said, "I wouldn't. I don't know what I'd do. Guess I just don't have a thieving mind."

"But somebody's doing it," he said. "Damned if I know what."

And we moved along at that steady fast trot, and my roan dropped back where he liked to stay, about twenty feet behind where he could set his own rhythm without being bothered trying to match the strides of the longer-legged bay. We moved along, and I began to feel empty clear down into my shanks and I began to hunch forwards to ease the callouses on my rump. The only break all morning was a short stop for brief watering. We moved along and into the afternoon, and I could tell the roan felt exactly as I did. He and I were concentrating on just one thing, putting all we had into following twenty feet after an old iron ramrod of a man on one of the long-legged, tireless horses of his own shrewd breeding.

The trail was still stale, several days at least, and we were not watching sharp ahead, so we came on them suddenly. Rodock, being ahead and going up a rise, saw them first and was swinging to the ground and grabbing his horse's nose when I came beside him and saw the herd, bunched, well ahead and into a small canyon that cut off to the right. I swung down and caught the roan's nose in time to stop the nicker starting, and we hurried to lead both horses back down the rise and a good ways more and over to a clump of trees. We tied them there and went ahead again on foot, crawling the last stretch up the rise and dropping on our bellies to peer over the top. They were there all right, the whole herd, the mares grazing quietly, some of the foals lying down, the others skittering around the way they do, daring each other to flip their heels.

We studied that scene a long time, checking every square yard of it as far as we could see. There was not a man or a saddled horse in sight. Rodock plucked a blade of grass and stuck it in his mouth and chewed on it.

"All right, son," he said. "Seems we'll have to smoke them out. They must be holed up somewhere handy waiting to see if anyone's following. You scout around the left side of that canyon and I'll take the right. Watch for tracks and keep an eye cocked behind you. We'll meet way up there beyond the herd where the trees and bushes give good cover. If you're jumped, get off a shot and I'll be on my way over ahumping."

"Mister Rodock," I said, "you do the same and so will I."

We separated, slipping off our different ways and moving slow behind any cover that showed. I went along the left rim of the canyon, crouching by rocks and checking the ground carefully each time before moving on and peering down into the canyon along the way. I came on a snake and circled it and flushed a rabbit out of some bushes, and those were the only living things or signs of them I saw except for the horses below there in the canyon. Well up beyond them, where the rock wall slanted out into a passable slope, I worked my way down and to where we were to meet. I waited, and after a while Rodock appeared, walking towards me without even trying to stay under cover.

"See anything, son?" he said.

"No," I said.

"It's crazier than ever," he said. "I found their tracks where they left. Three shod horses moving straight out. Now what made them chuck and run like that? Tracks at least a day old too."

"Somebody scared them," I said.

"It would take a lot," he said, "to scare men with nerve enough to make off with a bunch of my horses. Who'd be roaming around up here anyway? If it was anyone living within a hundred miles, they'd know my brand and be taking the horses in." He stood there straight, hands on his hips, and stared down the canyon at the herd. "What's holding them?" he said.

"Holding who?" I said.

"Those horses," he said. "Those mares. Why haven't they headed for home? Why aren't they working along as they graze?"

He was right. They weren't acting natural. They were bunched too close and hardly moving, and when any of them did move there was something wrong. We stared at them, and suddenly Rodock began to run towards them and I had trouble staying close behind him. They heard us and turned to face us and they had trouble turning, and Rodock stopped and stared at them and there was a funny moaning sound in his throat.

"My God!" he said. "Look at their front feet!"

I looked, and I could see right away what he meant. They had been roped and thrown and their front hooves rasped almost to the quick, so that they could barely put their weight on them. Each step hurt, and they couldn't have travelled at all off the canyon grass out on the rocky ground beyond. It hurt me seeing them hurt each time they tried to move, and if it did that to me I could imagine what it did to Jeremy Rodock.

They knew him, and some of them nickered at him, and the old mare that was their leader, and was standing with head drooping, raised her head and started forward and dropped her head again and limped to us with it hanging almost to the ground. There was a heavy iron bolt tied to her forelock and hanging down between her eyes. You know how a horse moves its head as it walks. This bolt would have bobbed against her forehead with each step she took, and already it had broken through the skin and worn a big sore that was beginning to fester.

Rodock stood still and stared at her and that moaning sound clung in his throat. I had to do something. I pulled out my pocket-knife and cut through the tied hair and tossed the bolt far as I could. I kicked up a piece of sod and reached down and took a handful of clean dirt and rubbed it over the sore on her forehead and then wiped it and the oozing stuff away with my neckerchief, and she stood for me and only shivered as I rubbed. I looked at Rodock and he was someone I had never seen before. He was a gaunt figure of a man, with eyes pulled back deep in their sockets and burning, and the bones of his face showing plain under the flesh.

"Mister Rodock," I said, "are we riding out on that three-horse trail?"

I don't think he even heard me.

"Not a thing," he said. "Not a single solitary goddamned thing I can do. They're travelling light and fast now. Too much of a start and too far up in the rocks for trailing. They've probably separated and could be heading clean out of the Territory. They're devilish smart and they've done it, and there's not a goddamned thing I can do."

"We've got the mares," I said. "And the foals."

He noticed me, a flick of his eyes at me. "We've got them way up here and they can't be moved. Not till those hooves grow out." He turned towards me and threw words at me, and I wasn't anyone he knew, just someone to be a target for his bitterness. "They're devils! Three devils! Nothing worth the name of man would treat horses like that. See the devilishness of it? They run my horses way up here and cripple them. They don't have to stay around. The horses can't get away. They know the chances are we won't miss the mares for weeks, and by then the trail will be overgrown and we won't know which way they went and waste time combing the whole damn country in every direction, and maybe never get up in here. Even if someone follows them soon, like we did, they're gone and can't be caught. One of them can slip back every week or two to see what's doing, and if he's nabbed what can tie him to the run-off? He's just a fiddlefoot riding through. By weaning-time, if nothing has happened, they can hurry in and take the colts and get off clean with a lot of unbranded horseflesh. And there's not a thing we can do."

"We can watch the mares," I said, "till they're able to travel some, then push them home by easy stages. And meantime be mighty rough on anyone comes noseying around."

"We've got the mares," he said. "They're as well off here as anywhere now. What I want is those devils. All three of them.

Together and roped and in my hands." He put out his hands, the fingers clawed, and shook them at me. "I've got to get them! Do you see that? I've got to!" He dropped his hands limp at his sides, and his voice dropped too, dry and quiet with a coldness in it. "There's one thing we can do. We can leave everything as it is and go home and keep our mouths shut and wait and be here when they come for the colts." He took hold of me by the shoulders and his fingers hurt my muscles. "You see what they did to my horses. Can you keep your mouth shut?"

He didn't wait for me to answer. He let go of my shoulders and turned and went straight through the herd of crippled mares without looking at them and on down the canyon and out and over the rise where we first sighted them and on to the clump of trees where we had tied our horses.

I followed him and he was mounted and already starting off when I reached the roan and I mounted and set out after him. He was in no hurry now and let the bay walk part of the time, and the roan and I were glad of that. He never turned to look at me or seemed to notice whether I followed or not. A rabbit jumped out of the brush and I knocked it over on the second shot and picked it up and laid it on the saddle in front of me, and he paid no attention to me, not even to the shots, just steadying the bay when it started at the sharp sounds and holding it firm on the back trail.

He stopped by a stream while there was still light and dismounted, and I did the same. After we had hobbled and unsaddled the horses, he sat on the ground with his back to a rock and stared into space. I couldn't think of anything to say, so I gathered some wood and made a fire. I took my knife and gutted the rabbit and cut off the head. I found some fairly good clay and moistened it and rolled the rabbit in a ball of it and dropped this in the fire. When I thought it would be about done, I poked it out of the hot ashes and let it cool a bit. Then I pried off the baked clay and the skin came with it and the meat showed juicy and smelled fine. It was still a little raw, but anything would have tasted good then. I passed Rodock some pieces and he took them and ate the meat off the bones mechanically like his mind was far away some place. I still couldn't think of anything to say, so I stretched out with my head on my saddle, and then it was morning and I was chilled and stiff and staring up at clear sky, and he was coming towards me leading both horses and his already saddled.

It was getting towards noon, and we were edging on to our home range when we met two of the regular hands out looking for us. They came galloping with a lot of questions and Rodock put up a palm to stop them.

"Nothing's wrong," he said. "I took a sudden mind to circle around and look over some of the stock that's strayed a bit and show the boy here parts of my range he hadn't seen before. Went farther'n I intended to and we're some tuckered. You two cut over to the lower basin and take in a pair of four-year-olds. Hightail it straight and don't dawdle. We've got that stage order to meet."

They were maybe a mite puzzled as they rode off, but it was plain they hadn't hit the second basin and seen the mares were missing. Rodock and I started on, and I thought of something to say and urged the roan close.

"Mister Rodock," I said, "I don't like that word 'boy.'"

"That's too damn bad," he said, and went steadily on and I followed, and he paid no more attention to me all the rest of the way to the ranch buildings.

Things were different after that around the place. He didn't work with the horses himself anymore. Most of the time he stayed in his sturdy frame house where he had a Mexican to cook for him and fight the summer dust, and I don't know what he did in there.

Once in a while he'd be on the porch, and he'd sit there hours staring off where the foothills started their climb towards the mountains. With him shut away like that, I was paired with Hugh Claggett. This Claggett was a good enough man, I guess. Rodock thought some of him. They had knocked around together years back, and when he had showed up needing a job sometime before I was around the place, Rodock gave him one, and he was a sort of acting foreman when Rodock was away for any reason. He knew horses, maybe as much as Rodock himself in terms of the things you could put down as fact in a book. But he didn't have the real feel, the deep inside feel, of them that means you can sense what's going on inside a horse's head; walk up to a rolled-eye maverick that's pawing the sky at the end of a rope the way Rodock could, and talk the nonsense out of him and have him standing there quivering to quiet under your hand in a matter of minutes. Claggett was a precise, practical sort of a man, and working with him was just that, working, and I took no real pleasure in it.

When Rodock did come down by the stables and working corral, he was different. He didn't come often, and it would have been better if he hadn't come at all. First thing I noticed was his walk. There was no bounce to it. Always before, no matter how tired he was, he walked rolling on the soles of his feet from heels to toes and coming off the toes each step with a little bouncy spring. Now he was walking flatfooted, plodding, like he was carrying more weight than just his body. And he was hard and driving in a new way, a nasty and irritable way. He'd always been one to find fault, but that had been because he was better at his business than any of us and he wanted to set us straight. He'd shrivel us down to size with a good clean tongue-whipping, then pitch in himself and show us how to do whatever it was and we'd be the better for it. Now he was plain cussed all through. He'd snap at us about anything and everything. Nothing we did was right. He'd not do a lick of work himself, just stand by and find fault, and his voice was brittle, and nasty, and he'd get personal in his remarks. And he was mighty touchy about how we treated the horses. We did the way he had taught us and the way I knew was right by how the horses handled, still he would blow red and mad and tear into us with bitter words, saying we were slapping on leather too hard or fitting bridles too snug, little things, but they added to a nagging tally as the days passed and made our work tiring and troublesome. There was a lot of grumbling going on in the bunkhouse in the evenings.

Time and again I wanted to tell the others about the mares so maybe they would understand. But I'd remember his hands stretching towards me and shaking and then biting into my shoulders and I'd keep what had happened blocked inside me. I knew what was festering in him. I'd wake at night thinking about those mares, thinking about them way up there in the hills pegged to a small space of thinning grass by hooves that hurt when weight came on them and sent stabs of pain up their legs when they hit anything hard. A good horse is a fine-looking animal. But it isn't the appearance that gets into you and makes something in you reach out and respond to him. It's the way he moves, the sense of movement in him even when he's standing still, the clean-stepping speed and competence of him that's born in him and is what he is and is his reason for being. Take that away and he's a pitiful thing. And somewhere there were three men who had done that to those mares. I'd jump awake at night and think about them and maybe have some notion of what it cost Jeremy Rodock to stay set there at his ranch and leave his mares alone with their misery far off up in the hills.

When the stage horses were ready to be shod for the last real road tests, he nearly drove our blacksmith crazy cursing every time a hoof was trimmed or one of them flinched under the hammer. We finished them off with hard runs in squads hitched to the old coach and delivered them, and then there was nothing much to do. Not another order was waiting. Several times agents had been to see Rodock and had gone into the house and come out again and departed, looking downright peeved. I don't know whether he simply refused any more orders or acted so mean that they wouldn't do business with him. Anyway, it was bad all around. There was too much loafing time. Except for a small crew making hay close in, no one was sent out on the range at all. The men were dissatisfied and they had reason to be, and they took to quarrelling with each other. Some of them quit in disgust and others after arguing words with Rodock, and finally the last bunch demanded their time together and left, and Claggett and I were the only ones still there. That's not counting the Mexican, but he was housebroke and not worth counting. Claggett and I could handle the chores for the few horses kept regularly around the place and still have time to waste. We played euchre, but I never could beat him and then got tired of trying. And Rodock sat on his porch and stared into the distance. I didn't think he even noticed me when I figured that his bay would be getting soft and started saddling him and taking him out for exercise the same as I did the roan. One day I rode him right past the porch. Rodock fooled me on that, though. I was almost past, pretending not to see him, when his voice flicked at me. "Easy on those reins, boy. They're just extra trimming. That horse knows what you want by the feel of your legs around him. I don't want him spoiled." He was right too. I found you could put that bay through a figure eight or drop him between two close-set posts just by thinking it down through your legs.

The slow days went by, and I couldn't stand it any longer. I went to the house.

"Mister Rodock," I said, "it's near two months now. Isn't it time we made a move?"

"Don't be so damn young," he said. "I'll move when I know it's right."

I stood on one foot and then on the other and I couldn't think of anything to say except what I'd said before about my age, so I went back to the bunkhouse and made Claggett teach me all the games of solitaire he knew.

Then one morning I was oiling harness to keep it limber when I looked up and Rodock was in the stable doorway.

"Saddle my bay," he said, "and Hugh's sorrel. I reckon that roan'll do for you again. Pick out a good packhorse and bring them all around to the storehouse soon as you can."

I jumped to do what he said, and when I had the horses there he and Claggett had packs filled. We loaded the extra horse, and the last thing Rodock did was hand out Henrys and we tucked these in our saddle scabbards and started out. He led the way, and from the direction he took it was plain we were not heading straight into the hills, but were going to swing around and come in from the south.

I led the packhorse and we rode in a compact bunch, not pushing for speed. It was in the afternoon that we ran into the other riders, out from the settlement and heading our way, Ben Kern, who was federal marshal for that part of the Territory, and three of the men he usually swore in as deputies when he had a need for any. We stopped and they stopped, looking us over.

"You've saved me some miles," Kern said. "I was heading for your place."

Rodock raised his eyebrows and looked at him and was silent.

I kept my mouth shut. Claggett, who probably knew as much about the mares as I did by now, did the same. This was Rodock's game.

"Not saying much, are you?" Kern said. He saw the Henrys. "Got your war paint on too. I thought something would be doing from what I've been hearing about things at your place. What's on your mind this time?"

"My mind's my own," Rodock said. "But it could be we're off on a little camping trip."

"And again it couldn't," Kern said. "Only camping you ever do is on the tail of a horse thief. That's the trouble. Twice now you've ridden in to tell me where to find them swinging. Evidence was clear enough, so there wasn't much I could do. But you're too damn free with your rope. How we going to get decent law around here with you old timers crossing things up? This time, if it is a this time, you're doing it right and turn them over to me. We'll just ride along to see that you do it."

Rodock turned to me. He had that grim and enduring look and the lines by his mouth were taut. "Break out those packs, boy. We're camping right here." I saw what he was figuring and I dismounted and began unfastening the packs. I had them on the ground and was fussing with the knots when Kern spoke.

"You're a stubborn old devil," he said. "You'd stay right here and outwit us."

"I would," Rodock said.

"All right," Kern said. "We'll fade. But I've warned you. If it's rustlers you're after, bring them to me."

Rodock didn't say a thing and I heaved the packs on the horse again, and by time I had them fastened tight, Kern and his men were a distance away and throwing dust. We started on, and by dark we had gone a good piece. By dark the next day we had made a big half-circle and were well into the hills. About noon of the next, we were close enough to the canyon where we had found the mares, say two miles if you could have hopped it straight. Claggett and I waited while Rodock scouted around. He came back and led us up a twisting rocky draw to a small park hemmed in part way by a fifteen-foot rock shelf and the rest of the way by a close stand of pine. It was about a half-acre in size, and you'd never know it was there unless you came along the draw and stumbled into it. We picketed the horses there and headed for the canyon on foot, moving slow and cautious as we came close. When we peered over the rim, the herd was there all right, the foals beginning to get some growth and the mares stepping a lot easier than before. They were used to the place now and not interested in leaving. They had taken to ranging pretty far up the canyon, but we managed to sight the whole count after a few minutes' watching.

We searched along the rim for the right spot and found it, a crack in the rim wide enough for a man to ease into comfortably and be off the skyline for anyone looking from below, yet able to see the whole stretch where the herd was. To make it even better, we hauled a few rocks to the edge of the opening and piled brush with them, leaving a careful spy-hole. The idea was that one of us could sit there watching while the other two holed in a natural hiding-place some fifty feet back under an overhanging ledge with a good screen of brush. The signal, if anything happened, was to be a pebble chucked back towards the hiding-place.

I thought we'd take turns watching, but Rodock settled on that flat-top stone and froze there. Claggett and I kept each other company under the ledge, if you could call it keeping company when one person spent most of the time with his mouth shut whittling endless shavings off chunks of old wood or taking naps. That man Claggett had no nerves. He could keep his knife going for an hour at a time without missing a stroke or stretch out and drop off into a nap like we were just lazing around at the ranch. He didn't seem to have much personal interest in what might develop. He was just doing a job and tagging along with an old-time partner. As I said before, he didn't have a real feel for horses. I guess to be fair to him I ought to remember that he hadn't seen those mares with their hooves rasped to the quick and flinching and shuddering with every step they took. Me, I was strung like a too-tight fiddle. I'd have cracked sure if I hadn't had the sense to bring a deck in my pocket for solitaire. I nearly wore out those cards and even took to cheating to win, and it seemed to me we were cooped there for weeks when it was only five days. And all the time, every day, Rodock sat on that stone as if he was a piece of it, getting older and grayer and grimmer.

Nights we spent back with the horses. We'd be moving before dawn each morning, eating a heavy breakfast cooked over a small quick fire, then slipping out to our places with the first streaks of light carrying a cold snack in our pockets. We'd return after dark for another quick meal and roll right afterwards into our blankets. You'd think we hardly knew each other the way we behaved, only speaking when that was necessary. Claggett was never much of a talker, and Rodock was tied so tight in himself now he didn't have a word to spare. I kept quiet because I didn't want him smacking my age at me again. If he could chew his lips and wear out the hours waiting, I could too, and I did.

We were well into the fifth day and I was about convinced nothing would ever happen again, any time ever anywhere in the whole wide world, when a pebble came snicking through the brush and Rodock came hard after it, ducking low and hurrying.

"They're here," he said. "All three." And I noticed the fierce little specks of light beginning to burn in his eyes. "They're stringing rope to trees for a corral. Probably planning to brand here, then run." He looked at me and I could see him assessing me and dismissing me, and he turned to Claggett. "Hugh," he started to say, "I want you to—"

I guess it was the way he had looked at me and the things he had said about my age. Anyway, I was mad. I didn't know what he was going to say, but I knew he had passed me by. I grabbed him by the arm.

"Mister Rodock," I said, "I'm the one rode with you after those mares."

He stared at me and shook his head a little as if to clear it.

"All right, boy," he said. "You do this and, by God, you do it right. Hurry back and get your horse and swing around and come riding into the canyon. Far as I can tell at the distance, these men are strangers, so there's not much chance they'd know you worked for me. You're just a drifter riding through. Keep them talking so Hugh and I can get down behind them. If they start something, keep them occupied long as you can." He grabbed me by the shoulders the way he had when we found the mares. "Any shooting you do, shoot to miss. I want them alive." He let go of me. "Now scat."

I scatted. I never went so fast over rough country on my own feet in my life. When I reached the roan, I had to hang on to his neck to get some breath and my strength back. I slapped my saddle on and took him at a good clip, but not too much to put him in a lather. I was heading into the canyon, pulling him to an easy trot, when it hit me, what a damn fool thing I was doing. There were three of them in there, three mighty smart men with a lot of nerve, and they had put a lot of time and waiting into this job and wouldn't likely be wanting to take chances on its going wrong. I was scared, so scared I could hardly sit the roan, and I came near swinging him around and putting my heels to him. Maybe I would have. Maybe I would have run out on those mares. But then I saw that one of the men had spotted me and there was nothing much to do but keep going towards them.

The one that had spotted me was out a ways from the others as a lookout. He had a rifle and he swung it to cover me as I came near and I stopped the roan. He was a hardcase specimen if ever I saw one and I didn't like the way he looked at me.

"Hold it now, sonny," he said. "Throw down your guns."

I was glad he said that, said "sonny," I mean, because it sort of stiffened me and I wasn't quite so scared, being taken up some with being mad. I tried to act surprised and hold my voice easy.

"Lookahere," I said, "that's an unfriendly way to talk to a stranger riding through. I wouldn't think of using these guns unless somebody pushed me into it, but I'd feel kind of naked without them. Let's just leave them alone, and if you're not the boss, suppose you let me talk to him that is."

I figured he wouldn't shoot because they'd want to know was I alone and what was I doing around there, and I was right. He jerked his head towards the other two.

"Move along, sonny," he said. "But slow. And keep your hands high in sight. I'll blast you out of that saddle if you wiggle a finger."

I walked the roan close to the other two and he followed behind me and circled around me to stand with them. They had been starting a fire and had stopped to stare at me coming. One was a short, stocky man, almost bald, with a fringe of grizzled beard down his cheeks and around his chin. The other was about medium height and slender, with clean chiseled features and a pair of the hardest, shrewdest, bluest eyes I ever saw. It was plain he was the boss by the way he took over. He set those eyes on me and I started shivering inside again.

"I've no time to waste on you," he said. "Make it quick. What's your story?"

"Story?" I said. "Why, simple enough. I'm footloose and roaming for some months and I get up this way with my pockets about played out. I'm riding by and I see something happening in here and I drop in to ask a few questions."

"Questions?" he said, pushing his head forward at me. "What kind of questions?"

"Why," I said, "I'm wondering maybe you can tell me, if I push on through these hills do I come to a town or some place where maybe I can get a job?"

The three of them stood there staring at me, chewing on this, and I sat in my saddle staring back, when the bearded man suddenly spoke.

"I ain't sure," he said, looking at the roan. "But maybe that's a Rodock horse."

I saw them start to move and I dove sideways off the roan, planning to streak for the brush, and a bullet from the rifle went whipping over the saddle where I'd been, and I hadn't more than bounced the first time when a voice like a chill wind struck the three of them still. "Hold it, and don't move!"

I scrambled up and saw them stiff and frozen, slowly swiveling their necks to look behind them at Rodock and Hugh Claggett and the wicked ready muzzles of their two Henrys.

"Reach," Rodock said, and they reached. "All right, boy," he said. "Strip them down."

I cleaned them thoroughly and got, in addition to the rifle and the usual revolvers, two knives from the bearded man and a small but deadly derringer from an inside pocket of the slender man's jacket.

"Got everything?" Rodock said. "Then hobble them good."

I did this just as thoroughly, tying their ankles with about a two-foot stretch between so they could walk short-stepped, but not run, and tying their wrists together behind their backs with a loop up and around their necks and down again so that if they tried yanking or pulling they'd be rough on their own Adam's apples.

They didn't like any of this. The slender man didn't say a word, just clamped his mouth and talked hate with his eyes, but the other two started cursing.

"Shut up," Rodock said, "or we'll ram gags down your throats." They shut up, and Rodock motioned to me to set them in a row on the ground leaning against a fallen tree and he hunkered down himself facing them with his Henry across his lap. "Hugh," he said, without looking away from them, "take down those ropes they've been running and bring their horses and any of their stuff you find over here. Ought to be some interesting branding irons about." He took off his hat and set it on the ground beside him. "Hop your horse, boy," he said; "get over to our hideout and bring everything back here."

When I returned leading our other horses, the three of them were still right in a row leaning against the log and Rodock was still squatted on the ground looking at them. Maybe words had been passing. I wouldn't know. Anyway, they were all quiet then. The hardcase was staring at his own feet. The bearded man's eyes were roaming around and he had a sick look on his face. The slender man was staring right back at Rodock and his mouth was only a thin line in his face. Claggett was standing to one side fussing with a rope. I saw he was fixing a hangman's knot on it and had two others already finished and coiled at his feet. When I saw them I had a funny empty feeling under my belt and I didn't know why. I had seen a hanging before and never felt like that I guess I had some kind of a queer notion that just hanging those three wouldn't finish the whole thing right. It wouldn't stop me waking at night and thinking about those mares and their crippled hooves.

My coming seemed to break the silence that had a grip on the whole place. The slender man drew back his lips and spit words at Rodock.

"Quit playing games," he said. "Get this over with. We know your reputation."

"Do you?" Rodock said. He stood up and waggled each foot in turn to get the kinks out of his legs. He turned and saw what Claggett was doing and a strange little mirthless chuckle sounded in his throat. "You're wasting your time, Hugh," he said. "We won't be using those. I'm taking these three in."

Claggett's jaw dropped and his mouth showed open. I guess he was seeing an old familiar pattern broken and he didn't know how to take it. I wasn't and I had caught something in Rodock's tone. I couldn't have said what it was, but it was sending tingles through my hair roots.

"Don't argue with me, Hugh," Rodock said. "My mind's set. You take some of the food and start hazing the herd towards home. They can do it now if you take them by easy stages. The boy and I'll take these three in."

I helped Claggett get ready and watched him go up the canyon to bunch the herd and get it moving. I turned to Rodock and he was staring down the back trail.

"Think you could handle four horses on lead ropes, boy?" he said. "The packhorse and their three."

"Expect I could, strung out," I said. "But why not split them? You take two and I take two."

"I'll be doing something else," he said, and that same little cold

28

chuckle sounded in his throat. "How far do you make it, boy, to the settlement and Kern's office?"

"Straight to it," I said, "I make it close to fifty mile."

"About right," he said. "Kind of a long hike for those used to having horses under them. Hop over and take the hobbles off their feet."

I hopped, but not very fast. I was feeling some disappointed. I was feeling that he was letting me and those mares down. A fifty-mile hike for those three would worry them plenty, and they'd be worrying too, about what would come at the end of it. Still it was a disappointment to think about

"While you're there," Rodock said, "pull their boots off too."

I swung to look at him. He was a big man, as I said before, but I'd run across others that stood taller and filled a doorway more, but right then he was the biggest man I ever saw anywhere any time in my whole life.

I didn't bother to take off the hobbles. I left them tied so they'd hold the boots together in pairs and I could hand them flapping over the back of the packhorse. I pulled the boots off, not trying to be gentle, just yanking, and I had a little trouble with the hard-case. He tried to kick me, so I heaved on the rope between his ankles and he came sliding out from the log flat on his back and roughing his bound hands under him, and after that he didn't try anything more. But what I remember best about the three of them then is the yellow of the socks the slender man wore. Those on the others were the usual dark gray, but his were bright yellow. I've thought about them lots of times and never been able to figure why and where he ever got them.

Rodock was rummaging in their stuff that Claggett had collected. He tossed a couple of branding irons towards me. "Bring these along," he said. "Maybe Kern will be interested in them." He picked up a whip, an old but serviceable one with a ten-foot lash, and tested it with a sharp crack. "Get up," he said to the three, and they got up. "I'll be right behind you with this. You'll stay bunched and step right along. Start walking."

They started, and he tucked his Henry in his saddle scabbard and swung up on the bay.

By time I had the other horses pegged in a line with the pack-horse as an anchor at the end and was ready to follow, they were heading out of the canyon and I hurried to catch up. I had to get out of the way, too, because Claggett had the herd gathered and was beginning to push the mares along with the foals skittering around through the bushes. Anyone standing on the canyon edge looking down would have seen a queer sight, maybe the damndest procession that ever paraded through that lonesome country. Those three were out in front, walking and putting their feet down careful even in the grass to avoid pebbles and bits of deadwood, with Rodock big and straight on his bay behind them, then me with my string of three saddled but riderless horses and the pack-horse, and behind us all the mares and the skittering foals with Claggett weaving on his sorrel to keep the stragglers on the move.

Once out of the canyon we had to separate. Rodock and I and our charges turned south-east to head for the settlement. Claggett had to swing the herd towards the north-east to head for the home range. He had his trouble with the mares because they wanted to follow me and my string. But he and his sorrel knew their business and by hard work made the break and held it. I guess he was a bit huffy about the whole thing because I waved when the distance was getting long between us, and he saw me wave and didn't even raise an arm. I don't know as I blame him for that.

This was mid-afternoon and by camping time we had gone maybe ten miles and had shaken down to a steady grind. My horses had bothered the roan some by holding back on the rope and had bothered themselves a few times by spread-eagling and trying to go in different directions, but by now the idea had soaked in and they were plugging along single-file and holding their places. The three men out in front had learned to keep moving or feel the whip. The slender man stepped along without paying attention to the other two and never looked back at Rodock and never said a word. The bearded man had found that shouting and cursing simply wore out his throat and had no effect on the grim figure pacing behind them. The hardcase had tried a break, ducking quick to one side and running fast as he could, but Rodock had jumped the bay and headed him the same as you do a steer, and being awkward with his hands tied he had taken a nasty tumble. Not a one of them was going to try that again. Their feet were too tender for hard running, anyway, especially out there in the open where the grass was bunchy with bare spaces aplenty, and there were stretches with a kind of coarse gravel underfoot. When Rodock called a halt by water, they were ready to flop on the ground immediately and hitch around and dabble their feet in the stream, and I noticed that the bottoms of their socks were about gone and the soles of their feet were red where they showed in splotches through the dirt ground in. I enjoyed those ten miles, not with a feeling of fun, but with a sort of slow, steady satisfaction.

I prepared food and Rodock and I ate, and then we fed them, one at a time. Rodock sat watch with his Henry on his lap while I untied them and let them eat and wash up a bit and tied them again. We pegged each of them to a tree for the night, sitting on the ground with his back to the trunk and a rope around so he wouldn't topple when he slept. I was asleep almost as soon as I stretched out, and I slept good, and I think Rodock did too.

The next day was more of the same except that we were at it a lot longer, morning and afternoon, and our pace slowed considerably as the day wore on. They were hard to get started again after a noon stop and the last hours before we stopped, they were beginning to limp badly. They weren't thinking anymore of how to make a break. They were concentrating on finding the easiest spots on which to set each step. I figured we covered twenty miles, and I got satisfaction out of every one of them. But the best were in the morning because along late in the afternoon I began to feel tired, not tired in my muscles but tired and somehow kind of shrinking inside. When we stopped, I saw that their socks were just shredded yarn around their ankles and their feet were swelling and angry red and blistery through the dirt. With them sullen and silent and Rodock gray and grim and never wasting a word, I began to feel lonesome, and I couldn't go to sleep right away and found myself checking and rechecking in my mind how far we had come and how many miles we still had to go.

The day after that we started late because there was rain during the night and we waited till the morning mists cleared. The dampness in the ground must have felt better to their feet for a while because they went along fairly good the first of the morning after we got under way. They were really hard to get started, though, after the noon stop. During the afternoon they went slower and slower, and Rodock had to get mean with the whip around the heels of the hardcase and the bearded man. Not the slender one. That one kept his head high and marched along and you could tell he was fighting not to wince with every step. After a while, watching him, I began to get the feel of him. He was determined not to give us the satisfaction of seeing this get to him in any serious way. I found myself watching him too much, too closely, so I dropped behind a little more, tagging along in the rear with my string, and before Rodock called the halt by another stream, I began to see the occasional small red splotches in the footprints on dusty stretches that showed the blisters on their feet were breaking. The best I could figure we had come maybe another ten miles during the day, the last few mighty slow. That made about forty altogether, and when I went over it in my mind I had to call it twelve more to go because we had curved off the most direct route some to avoid passing near a couple of line cabins of the only other ranch in that general neighborhood north of the settlement.

There weren't many words in any of us as we went through the eating routine. I didn't know men's faces were capable of such intense hatred as showed plain on the hardcase and the bearded man. They gobbled their food and glared at Rodock from their night-posts against trees, and for all I know glared without stopping all night because they had the same look the next morning. It was the slender man who suddenly took to talking. The hatred he'd had at the start seemed to have burned away. What was left was a kind of hard pride that kept his eyes alive. He looked up from his food at Rodock.

"It was a good try," he said.

"It was," Rodock said. "But not good enough. Your mistake was hurting my horses."

"I had to," the man said. "That was part of it. I saw some of your horses on a stage line once. I had to have a few."

"If you wanted some of my horses," Rodock said, "why didn't you come and buy them?"

"I was broke," the man said.

"You were greedy," Rodock said. "You had to take all in that basin. If you'd cut out a few and kept on going, you might have made it."

"Maybe," the man said. "Neither of us will ever know now. You planning to keep this up all the way in?"

"I am," Rodock said.

"Then turn us over?" the man said.

"Yes," Rodock said.

"You're the one that's greedy," the man said.

He shut up and finished his food and crawled to his tree and refused to look at Rodock again. I fixed his rope and then I had trouble getting to sleep. I lay a long time before I dozed and what sleep I got wasn't much good.

In the morning Rodock was gray and grimmer than ever before. Maybe he hadn't slept much either. He stood off by himself and let me do everything alone. I couldn't make the hardcase and the bearded man get on their feet, and I found my temper mighty short and was working up a real mad when the slender man, who was up and ready, stepped over and kicked them, kicked them with his own swollen feet that had the remains of his yellow socks flapping around the ankles.

"Get up!" he said. "Damn you, get up! We're going through with this right!"

They seemed a lot more afraid of him than of me. They staggered up and they stepped along with him as Rodock came close with the whip in his hand and we got our pathetic parade started again. We couldn't have been moving much more than a mile an hour, and even that pace slowed, dropping to about a crawl when we hit rough stretches, and more and more red began to show in the footprints. And still that slender man marched along, slow but dogged, the muscles in his neck taut as he tried to stay straight without wincing.

Rodock was mean and nasty, crowding close behind them, using the whip to raise the dust around the lagging two. I didn't like the look of him. The skin of his face was stretched too tight and his eyes were too deep-sunk. I tried riding near him and making a few remarks to calm him, but he snapped at me like I might be a horse thief myself, so I dropped behind and stayed there.

He didn't stop at noontime, but kept them creeping along, maybe because he was afraid he'd never get them started again. It was only a short while after that the bearded man fell down, just crumpled and went over sideways and lay still. It wasn't exactly a faint or anything quite like that. I think he had cracked inside, had run out his score and quit trying, even trying to stay conscious. He was breathing all right, but it was plain he wouldn't do any more walking for a spell.

Rodock sat on his horse and looked down at him. "All right, boy," he said. "Hoist him on one of your string and tie him so he'll stay put." I heaved him on the first of the horses behind me and slipped a rope around the horse's barrel to hold him. Rodock sat on his bay and looked at the other two men, not quite sure what to do, and the slender one stared back at him, contempt sharp on his face, and Rodock shook out the whip. "Get moving, you two!" he said, and we started creeping along again.

It was about another hour and maybe another mile when the hardcase began screaming. He threw himself on the ground and rolled and thrashed and kept screaming, then stretched out taut and suddenly went limp all over, wide awake and conscious, but staring up as if he couldn't focus on anything around him.

Rodock had to stop again, chewing his lower lip and frowning. "All right, boy," he said. "Hoist that one too." I did, the same as the other one, and when I looked around, damned if that slender man wasn't walking on quite a distance ahead with Rodock right behind him.

I didn't want to watch, but I couldn't help watching that man stagger on. I think he had almost forgotten us. He was intent on the terrible task of putting one foot forward after the other and easing his weight on to it. Rodock, bunched on his bay and staring at him, was the one who cracked first. The sun was still up the sky, but he shouted a halt and when the man kept going he had to jump down and run ahead and grab him. It was a grim business making camp. The other two had straightened out some, but they had no more spirit in them than a pair of limp rabbits. I had to lift them down, and it wasn't until they had some food in them that they began to perk up at all. They seemed grateful when I hiked a ways and brought water in a folding canvas bucket from one of the packs and let them take turns soaking their swollen bloody feet in it. Then I took a saddle blanket and ripped it in pieces and wrapped some of them around their feet. I think I did that so I wouldn't find myself always sneaking looks at their feet. I did the same for the slender man, and all the time I was doing it he looked at me with that contempt on his face and I didn't give a damn. I did this even though I thought Rodock might not like it, but he didn't say a word. I noticed he wouldn't look at me and I found I didn't want to look at him either. I tried to keep my mind busy figuring how far we had come and made it six miles with six more still to go, and I was wishing those six would fade away and the whole thing would be over. The sleep I got that night wasn't worth anything to me.

In the morning I didn't want any breakfast and I wasn't going to prepare any unless Rodock kicked me into it He was up ahead of me, standing quiet and chewing his lower lip and looking very old and very tired, and he didn't say a word to me. I saddled the horses the way I had been every morning because that was the easiest way to tote the saddles along and tied them in the usual string. The slender man was awake, watching me, and by time I finished the other two were too. They were thoroughly beaten. They couldn't have walked a quarter of a mile with the devil himself herding them. I thought to hell with Rodock and led the horses up close and hoisted the two, with them quick to help, into their saddles. They couldn't put their feet in the stirrups, but they could sit the saddles and let their feet dangle. I went over to the slender man and started to take hold of him, and he glared at me and shook himself free of my hands and twisted around and strained till he was up on his feet. I stood there gaping at him and he hobbled away, heading straight for the settlement. I couldn't move. I was sort of frozen inside watching him. He made about fifty yards and his legs buckled under him. The pain in his feet must have been stabbing up with every step and he simply couldn't stand any longer. And then while I stared at him he started crawling on his hands and knees.

"God damn it, boy!" Rodock's voice behind me made me jump. "Grab that man! Haul him back here!"

I ran and grabbed him and after the first grab, he didn't fight and I hauled him back. "Hoist him on his horse," Rodock said, and I did that. And then Rodock started cursing. He cursed that man and he cursed me and then he worked back over us both again. He wasn't a cursing man and he didn't know many words and he didn't have much imagination at it, but what he did know he used over and over again and after a while he ran down and stopped and chewed his lower lip. He turned and stalked to the packhorse and took the pairs of tied boots and came along the line tossing each pair over the withers of the right horse. He went back to the packs and pulled out the weapons I'd found on the three and checked to see that the guns were empty and shook the last of the flour out of its bag and put the weapons in it with the rifle barrel sticking out the top. He tied the bag to the pommel of the slender man's saddle.

"All right, boy," he said. "Take off those lead ropes and untie their hands."

When I had done this and they were rubbing their wrists, he stepped close to the slender man's horse and spoke up at the man.

"Back to the last creek we passed yesterday," he said, "and left along it a few miles you come to Shirttail Fussel's shack. From what I hear for a price he'll hide out anything and keep his mouth shut. A man with sense would fix his feet there and then keep travelling and stay away from this range the rest of his days."

The slender man didn't say a word. He pulled his horse around and started in the direction of the creek and the other two tagged him, and what I remember is that look of hard pride still in his eyes, plain and sharp against the pinched and strained bleakness of his face.

We watched them go and I turned to Rodock. He was old, older even than I thought he was when I first saw him, and tired with heavy circles under his eyes. At that moment I didn't like him at all, not because he had let them go, but because of what he had put me through, and it was my turn to curse him. I did it right. I did a better job than he had done before and he never even wagged a muscle. "Shut up," he said finally. "I need a drink." He went to his bay and mounted and headed for the settlement. I watched him, hunched forward and old in the saddle, and I was ashamed. I took the lead rope of the packhorse and climbed on the roan and followed him. I was glad when he put the bay into a fast trot because I was fed up with sitting on a walking horse.

He bobbed along ahead of me, a tired old man who seemed too small for that big bay, and then a strange thing began to happen. He began to sit straighter in the saddle and stretch up and look younger by the minute, and when we reached the road and headed into the settlement he was Jeremy Rodock riding straight and true on a Rodock horse and riding it like it was the part of him that in a way it really was. He hit a good clip the last stretch and my roan and the packhorse were see-sawing on the lead rope trying to keep up when we reached the buildings and pulled in by a tie-rail. I swung down right after him and stepped up beside him and we went towards the saloon. We passed the front window of Kern's office and he was inside and came popping out.

"Hey, you two," he said. "Anything to report?"

We stopped and faced him and he looked at us kind of funny. I guess we did look queer, dirty and unshaved and worn in spots.

"Not a thing," Rodock said. "I told you we could be taking a camp trip and that's all I'll say. Except that I'm not missing any stock and haven't stretched any rope."

We went into the saloon and to the bar and downed a stiff one apiece.

"Mister Rodock," I said, "when you think about it, that man beat us."

"Damned if he didn't," Rodock said. He didn't seem to be bothered by it and I know I wasn't. "Listen to me, son," he said. "I expect I haven't been too easy to get along with for quite a few weeks lately. I want you to know I've noticed how you and that roan have stuck to my heels over some mighty rough trail. Now we've got to get home and get a horse ranch moving again. We'll be needing some hands. Come along with me, son, and we'll look around. I'd like your opinion on them before hiring any."

That was Jeremy Rodock. They don't grow men like that around here anymore.

Miley Bennett

In the morning I saddled the gray and rode into town, not hurrying because I didn't like what I was going to do. But I had thought this all out after the trial was over, and I couldn't see any other answer that would let me sleep at night.

There was a chill in the air and that was good because I could be wearing my blue denim jacket and no one would think that strange. As a matter of fact, few people were stirring on the street and not a one paid attention to me at all.

I stepped on the low porch of the solid frame building that served as marshal's office and jail. I opened the door and went through and to the railing that sliced the front room in half. Marshal Eakins sat at his rolltop desk behind it, finishing a cup of coffee from the pot topping the one-burner oil stove on a table in the right corner.

"Morning, John," he said. "Think I'll have another cup. Join me?"

I shook my head.

"Don't take to drinking alone," he said. "Not even coffee. Company tangs it better."

I shook my head again.

"First time in here for you, John," he said. "Bringing me business?"

"No," I said. "I just want to go in there and talk to him."

Eakins seemed surprised. "Funny company for you to be keeping," he said.

"It's a free country," I said.

"Damned if it ain't," he said. "You can have five minutes. So the rules say."

I swung the little gate and went through.

"Before you go in," he said, "I'll have to relieve you of this." He lifted the jacket on my right side and slipped the gun out of the holster and laid it on his desk. "No weapons inside," he said, unlocking the door to the back part of the building. "Except on me or a sworn deputy."

He led to the middle of the three barred cubicles and unlocked this and let me in and locked it again after me.

"Not too particular about time," he said. "A little hazy on how long is five minutes. Whistle if you want out sooner."

I stood with my back to the bars until he was out in the front room again. Miley Bennett sat on a stool below the lone high little window of the back wall. He was staring at the floor and he needed a shave, looking smaller and more meagre and burnt-eyed than the day before at the trial, and he was staring at the floor.

I sat on the bunk slung by straps from the right-side bars. He was staring at the floor, his eyes following a split in one of the planks, along and back, along and back.

"There's a new man out on the range, Miley," I said. "He's rounding up what's left of them, going to drive them over to the Association's spread near Meeteetsee where they'll be safe. He's treating them right."

He wouldn't say a word to me. You couldn't tell he even knew

I was there. I lifted the straw-stuffed burlap pillow and put the gun under it, the one I had hanging on a cord around my shoulder and under my left arm beneath the blue denim jacket. I patted the pillow and I saw his eyes flick over quickly at my hands and go back to the crack in the thick plank.

I went to the front bars and whistled. Eakins came and let me out and led to the front room, locking the door again behind us. He handed me the gun from the desk and I slipped it into the holster.

"Changed your mind about the coffee?" he said.

"No," I said. I went outside and swung up on the gray and started home. The sun was a little higher up the sky and the air was warming. I took off the jacket and folded it and tucked it under the front of the saddle.

Yes, I gave Miley Bennett the gun.

But, then, I knew what he would do with it.

∾⋮∾

I guess you'll have to let me tell this in my own way. There's no one else can tell it, not so it comes out right. I guess I'll just have to hope you understand what I mean. And how I felt.

The first time I saw Miley Bennett he was jogging steadily along my inner fence line on his burro. Small as he was, he was oversize on the tiny beast. I had just finished washing the supper dishes, plate and cup, and stepped out on the porch of my two-room frame ranch house and I saw him, legs almost dragging, head bouncing.

He came right up to the house, slid off the burro, stepped on the porch, straightened the whole five-foot—well, maybe five-foot two or three of him and grinned at me.

"The name is Bennett," he said. "Miley Bennett. Have you got any tobacco about the place?"

I had. And I had enough politeness or plain curiosity to ask this pint-size package of queer humanity in to smoke a pipeful with me. Things got mighty lonesome when your nearest neighbor was some two miles away and you were working hard to get a place in shape so you could have it ready and stock it before winter came down out of the mountains.

He was a talker, the first and only of his kind I ever knew to be. In half an hour I had a good handful of facts.

He was a sheepherder. He was herding sheep for one of the Association outfits with headquarters at Thermopolis. They had outfitted him and sent him off with a flock of eight hundred to graze them all spring and summer on government range. He was new at it then, so new that he took the job. It was four months later now, and he had worked his way, as near as I could judge from his talk, to a valley five miles above my place. The supply wagon that was supposed to stop by every six weeks or so was overdue. He had run out of tobacco two days ago and stood it as long as he could. He had left the sheep bedded for the night with the dogs and poked the burro into taking him in search of some he could borrow and someone who might bring him a supply from a next trip to the nearest town.

Some queer instinct must have headed him in my direction, kept him from the other places he might have hit. He certainly was an innocent one.

Half an hour seemed to be all he would allow himself. Call it one good pipeful. With a pokebag packed from my canister in his pocket and a promise I would have a supply soon in his mind, he became fidgety and stopped looking straight at me when he talked.

"Got to be going," he blurted suddenly. "Got to be getting back quick as I can."

"It'll be full dark before you get there," I said. "Are you sure you can find the way?"

He was at the door. "I'll find it. Or Beulah will. She can always find her way back to camp." He looked at me quickly and away. "You see, I've got to. The sheep are depending on me. I told them I'd be back early."

I listened to the soft little hoofbeats dropping away in the dusk and I thought of that funny frog-faced little man riding his burro through strange country in the darkness. And I began to realize just how innocent he was.

He probably thought he had a good job, was getting good pay. The pay part at least would be right. Members of the Sheepmen's Association were paying good wages for herders—when they could get them. They had to. Few men who knew what was what would take on the work at any price. Not in this section of the newly organized State where the cattlemen had been running beef stock, mostly on wide open range, for plenty of years and had dominant influence all along the line. Most cattlemen hated sheep and anyone who had anything to do with them, claimed they ruined the range. Sheep ate the grass, crown and all, right down to the roots, not just cropping the way cattle did, and they bunched together so closely and worked over the ground so thoroughly that when they moved on it was mighty bare, knocked out for the rest of the season. Some ranchers said they left a bad smell in the ground so that cattle would never go back where they had grazed. I think that was exaggerated, but shows how far some men would go in their thinking.

Sheep didn't bother me. I was a newcomer to this Territory with some fairly new ideas. I knew the open range wouldn't last, would be taken over by homesteaders and carved up by the creeping fence lines. I had seen it all happen before back in the Dakotas before I moved on to this new State of Wyoming. I knew you would make out better in the long run with a small herd held by fences, with your own pastures you could improve. You could control your breeding and feed right in the winter, get better grade stuff with hardly any losses. I had my land and my first fences. A consignment of low-slung Herefords would be along in about a month. The only thing I'd want from the open range would be some hay to add to that I'd clip from my own pasture. Sheep didn't worry me any.

They did worry the old-style ranchers. Worried them and made them mad. They had been running cattle in their own way a long time and didn't see any reason why they shouldn't keep right on as they always had. These men and their kind controlled the State Government. It didn't mean a thing to them that the free grass belonged to the Federal Government and that the Federal laws made no distinction between cattle and sheep. They did, and they intended to enforce it, and they had been finding ways. Sheep had been killed and flocks stampeded. I knew of two herders found dead back in the hills and several more beaten badly. Miley Bennett's was the only flock I had heard about anywhere around that year.

A week went past and he didn't appear. There was a three-pound can of tobacco waiting for him in the kitchen. It represented a cash outlay to me and I wanted to collect. Maybe that was why or maybe I was just plain curious again. Anyway, I saddled the gray late one afternoon, tied the can in a bag behind the saddle, tucked the Winchester in the worn scabbard, and rode out looking for him. I found him about where I figured. He was warming a can of beans over a wood fire and they smelled good and tasted the same.

The sheep were a hundred yards away where the ground was

packed like they had been spending the night there for quite a while. They were in a tight bunch with two dogs patrolling, one old and knowing and taking this easy, the other a youngster wasting energy and acting excited despite a noticeable limp. Miley was haggard like a man needing sleep. He seemed pleased to see me and not just for the tobacco.

"What's wrong with the dog?" I said when the coffee was in the tin cup he handed me.

"Murderers," he said. "Damn sneaking murderers. Wolves. They got three of my sheep the other night and damn near killed the one dog. The other one's a coward, must have stayed out of reach."

"He's not a coward," I said. "He's sensible. A wolf can kill a dog in about one slice. Have you seen them?"

"You bet I've seen them," he said. "Three of them. They came sneaking back the next night, last night. Not close enough for a shot, though. They won't get any more of my sheep. I won't let them. But I thought they weren't ever around this time of year."

"They come down out of the timber sometimes," I said. "There's a bounty on them. You want me to stay and see if we can scare them back tonight? Two guns are better than one." I was thinking of my own cattle coming. Wolves had a taste for calves. I was thinking he wouldn't be much good at this kind of thing and of the small shot-gun leaning against a nearby rock. A wolf would just laugh at a nuisance like that. He must have known what I was thinking.

"Hey, would you?" he said. "But let me show you something. I use that shotgun for snakes." He threw the empty bean can as far as he could out on the sod. He crawled into his little pup tent and came out with an old Army Hotchkiss. "I've been practicing ever since I started this job," he said.

He hit that can, a jagged chunk of tin bouncing farther away each time, four shots out of the five.

"You'll do," I said. "If you can do the same when your sights are down on a wolf."

He could all right. And he could lie absolutely quiet on his belly behind a boulder, patient as you had to be often in this country, for more than two hours on the windward side of the flock, which was the way the wolves would come. He drilled his clean, just behind the shoulder, and it dropped in its tracks. Mine stumbled with a broken leg and scrambled up and I had to pump in another shot quickly or it would have gotten away. The third one was off so fast, belly low and over a knoll, that we didn't have a chance at it.

"You won't have any trouble with that last one," I said when we had the ears and were back where the dogs were tied. "It'll head for the timber now."

Miley was so excited he could hardly settle down. He had to go over to his sheep and tell them all about it before he could sit by the fire I had got going again. Then he talked like he had a lot of words dammed inside him that had to break loose. I filled in behind the facts I already knew.

He was born and grew up back East in the factory badlands of New Jersey across the Hudson from the human beehives of Manhattan. His father was a factory hand and he was one of nine kids, and they rarely had full meals, and they lived on the streets as much as they did in the old tenement. He was the runt of the family. I guess he was slapped around plenty by his brothers as well as the neighborhood gang because he pulled out when he was sixteen and went on his own, setting pins in a bowling alley and living in a loft room the operator let him use.

After that he must have had a couple of dozen different jobs in nearly as many years, none of them amounting to much. He was just a little guy lost among the thousands of others, puttering through life and getting slapped around always by the bigger guys. The best job he ever had, he seemed to think, was as second bartender in a Newark saloon. His size didn't matter there. The other man was a husky brute who took a liking for him and could handle any trouble in the place without any help. Miley was working there when the coughing started and the doctor told him he'd not last long if he didn't head for a high dry climate.

The doctor meant some sanatorium. Miley had no money for anything like that, never had and never expected to have. It was the big bartender gave him the push. Fired him and handed him an extra week's pay and told him to keep going West till he reached the mountains, real mountains past the Mississippi and the prairie States.

He had reached Cheyenne the spring before, panhandling and picking up odd work on the way. A haying job nearly killed him, but carried him through the summer. Dishwashing in a scrubby hotel took him through the winter—and started the coughing again. The herding offer, spotted in a weekly paper, struck him like a miracle out of the blue. As near as I could gather, he had some silly notions about the noble life of the shepherd out in the great open spaces, all tied in somehow with some pictures he remembered from an early schoolbook. He still had them and he was proud that he hadn't lost a lamb all through the spring season.

He sat there by the fire talking and finally he talked himself out. The moon, a clear three-quarters moon, climbed over the far horizon and silvered the land, making pools of shadow between the rolls of the valley floor and shifting patterns of light and dark on the hills in front of the solid black of the soaring mountains beyond. The fire was only a few embers and I was trying to decide whether to saddle the gray or borrow one of his blankets for the night when he spoke.

"It's big, ain't it?" he said.

That was what it was. Big. You could use a lot of fancy words and never get anywhere as close as with that one little word.

"Makes a man feel big too," he said.

I stood up and started to walk around. Here was a funny frog-faced little runt from the worrying squirrel-cages of the eastern sea-board telling me for the first time, making me realize for the first time, why I was out in this Territory myself, why I had kept moving on out of the flat States till I found this Big Horn country.

I came back by the fire and I made my try. I tried to tell him what he was up against bringing sheep into this cow country and grazing them on the open range. I tried to tell him how the cow-men felt.

"That's all kind of silly," he said. "Look." He crawled into his pup tent again and scrooged around and came out with a paper pamphlet in his hand. "That's from the Government," he said. "You can't read it now, but I'll tell you about it. It's all about sheep raising. It says sheep eat things close down to the ground all right. But it says if you don't let them eat too long any one place, the grass comes back better than ever the next spring. That's the way I'm doing with them. It says that country like this up here is better for sheep than cows, anyway, because they'll eat stuff the cows won't and get more from every acre. It says they're more productive on rough range because they're two-crop animals, wool as well as lambs. Why, these cowmen you talk about would be better off if they took to sheep themselves."

"I won't argue that," I said. "I don't know enough. I just happen to like cows. They smell cleaner and they've got more sense."

"Oh, that's where you're wrong," he said. "Sheep don't smell bad after you get used to it. It's a kind of a warm nice smell on a chilly night. They've got lots of sense. They pick a leader and follow him. They get to know you and depend on you and do what you say. They'll listen to you and sometimes you get to understanding what they're saying back."

"Sounds crazy to me," I said. "But that's outside the argument. If you've got any sense yourself, you'll pack that burro and start moving yourself and your talking sheep far away."

"That's what the other fellow told me," he said. "Only he told me meaner."

"What other fellow?" I said.

"A big fellow on a black horse," he said. "They stopped by here two days ago."

"Must be Jeff Clayton," I said. "He has a lot of cattle on the range. He's not one to play games with. Are you taking his advice?"

"No," he said. "The man who hired me told me to come up this way and stay till September. My sheep aren't hurting anybody. I don't believe all that you've been telling me. People can't really act that way up here where it's so big. There's plenty of room for us all."

I was so peeved at the thick-headed little fool that I saddled the gray in the dark and rode home even though it was past midnight when I got there.

A couple of days later I took the ears into town and collected the bounty and for some reason on the way back Miley's share was burning a hole in my pocket, so I kept right on going. About noon when I headed into the valley I was surprised to see sheep scattered in little bunches in every direction.

The gray didn't like it much, and the sheep were slow and stupid, running in little spurts everywhere but where you wanted them to go, but I began herding them up the valley towards his camp. About half a mile coming over a knoll I saw him. He and the dogs were gathering them in, herding them into a single flock again. He was plodding along on foot and the dogs were racing after strays. He waved at me, grim-faced, and plodded on, and I kept my side closing in till the flock was about complete.

"What happened this time?" I said, dismounting to rest the gray.

"Horses," he said. "Lots of them. Wild ones. Worse murderers than those wolves. Before I got up this morning they came tearing. Ran right through my sheep. They trampled nine of them."

I pointed to one sheep whose left foreleg was dangling. "Better shoot that one," I said. "It won't be able to travel."

He looked at me like he thought I was out of my mind. "Shoot her? Shoot one of my sheep? I'll fix that leg with a splint. What do you mean travel?"

"If you've got a grain of sense," I said, "you'll be heading out of here now. There are no wild horses around here. Half-wild, maybe, but you'll find every one has a brand. And not even wild ones would stampede through a herd of sheep by themselves. Come on, I'll show you.",

We followed the trail of the hooves back up the valley a ways and at last off to one side a bit I found what I was looking for.

"See, Miley," I said, "that horse had shoes. It's being worked. Someone was riding it. Hunt around some more and probably we'd find more tracks."

He didn't say a word all the way back to his camp. He dug through his stuff and pulled out a small short miner's shovel.

"What's that for?" I said.

"I'm going to bury my sheep like I did the others," he said.

"You're the worst kind of a fool," I said. "You don't have to bury things out here. The buzzards take care of that. With that toy in this ground it would take you two whole days."

"No buzzards are getting my sheep," he said. He looked up at me, the whole little length of him shaking. "We're not getting out of here neither. I was pushed around enough back home. I'm not going to be pushed around here. We're going into that canyon on up there where there's good grass for a couple of weeks at least and I'm camping at the way in and nothing's going to get in to bother my sheep. Not with me there. I'll stay awake every night if I have to."

I quit trying then. I gave him his share of the bounty and I rode home, and I felt I had to call him plenty of hard names to myself all the way.

What happened after that isn't easy to tell. I can put it together fairly well because I knew Miley Bennett and heard him talk. The few words they got out of him at the trial helped some. What one of Jeff Clayton's men told, talking slow because of the bullet-hole in his shoulder, didn't mean much because he had to cover himself, but parts of it fitted the rest. Add all this to what I figured when I went over the ground the morning after it happened and you can fill in the whole thing. As I said before, I'll have to tell it in my own way. Small parts may be wrong, but the substance has to be right.

Miley Bennett buried his sheep and it took him at least the two days. He buried each in a separate grave and he lugged stones quite a distance to mark them. He got three buzzards with the shotgun while he was doing it. He herded the flock into the canyon, came back and packed everything tight on the burro and led her there too, and put his new camp in the neat order he liked. Two more days and nights went by and he slept only in snatches, watching the bigness of the dark land from his spy perch on a flat rock. Along about the middle of the morning of the third day there, he saw a man in the distance riding up the valley towards him. He climbed down from the rock and stepped behind, peering over the top with the shotgun ready in his right hand. He was watching the rider approach when a voice behind told him to drop the gun and reach for a piece of sky. He whirled and another man had come slipping quietly down the rocks and was there with a handkerchief tied over his face up to the eyes and a gun in his hand pointing straight at Miley's belt buckle. Miley was so startled that he couldn't make a move of his own while this one yanked the shotgun out of his grasp and sent him around the rock and into the open with a hard slap on the side of the head.

The rider came close and he too now had a handkerchief over his face. Then another man, a big man on a black horse with his handkerchief over his face, rode into sight down and around from the high rocks of the canyon top leading another horse.

The three of them were quiet and businesslike. The big man rode his horse right over the little pup tent, crushing it flat and trampling it. He dismounted and the other rider with him. They tied Miley Bennett to a tree facing up the canyon towards his grazing flock. Methodically they smashed everything in sight, the shotgun and the food bags and the cans of beans, even the can of tobacco. The big man stepped close to Miley Bennett. "Watch this," he said. "Then crawl back where you came from and tell every smelly sheep owner what happens to them in cattle country."

All three of them pulled high-powered rifles from their saddle scabbards and started towards the sheep. The first shots took the dogs. Then the bullets began ploughing into the flock, tearing through two and three bodies at a time. The sheep screamed their terror and scattered, running their short spurts and huddling in groups, and the bullets followed and ploughed into them. The rifle barrels were hot when the last shells were used and the men came for their horses and rode after the scattered remnants, trampling them as they could, chasing the terrified sheep in among the rocks and scrub growth of the canyon edges.

And all this while Miley Bennett, tight to torture against the tree, saw what he could not avoid seeing.

The men rode back and one dismounted to loosen the rope slightly and mounted again and they rode out of the canyon and down the valley and away.

~:~

Miley Bennett's mind climbed slowly back to consciousness out of a deep red darkness. It kept on climbing far above his surroundings, cool and detached from awareness of the immediate scene, unconcerned about his struggling body. He was alone with his dead and his wounded and his far-scattered living. The rope galls were deep in his arms and ankles and across his chest and he did not know it. Hours might have passed. It had really been perhaps twenty minutes.

His mind settled in a far niche and was quiet and a cold, clear logic flowed from it. He stopped struggling. He began to move in precise calculated lunges sidewise under the rope, edging around the tree trunk, oblivious of the rasping pull of the hemp along his body. When his fingers found the knot, his wrists bent at a grotesque upward angle, he picked slowly and steadily at it. When the rope loosened, his shoulders surged outward and the ends flipped free and he fell forward, wrenching his ankles on the lower coil that still held. When his feet were free, he crawled straight to the wrinkled, stomped canvas of the crushed pup tent.

Beneath the canvas in the sorry mess of the two blankets lay the old Hotchkiss. The stock was split with jagged splinters showing. The barrel and breech were intact. The last cartridge box was crumpled and broken, the cartridges pressed into the ground. He gathered as many as he could and cleaned them carefully and put them in his pockets. Standing up stiffly, he looked all around and whistled gently and then more loudly and saw a stirring in some far bushes. He limped there and made the snapped tether rope into a halter rein for the little burro. He pulled himself on her back and headed her out of the canyon and down the valley, holding the rope-rein in his left hand, the old Hotchkiss in his right hand.

He was no tracker and this was difficult for him. He found at last where the riders had swung off the main track through the valley and gone left through the rolling ridges and climbing foothills. The little burro plodded patiently and waited, head hanging, when he lost the trail and had to search in a circle for it. The sun was posting past noon when he topped the last rise and saw Clem Murphy's ranch house in its flat hollow and the three horses ground-reined in the shade of a tree by the corral.

He turned back below the top of the rise and slid off the little burro and tied her to a scrub tree. Back at the top, he lay on his belly and peered over and crawled carefully from bush to bush down the slope to a stack of weathering fence posts about a hundred yards from the house. He rubbed dirt on the barrel of the old Hotchkiss to remove any lingering metal glint and lay again on his belly behind the stack, peering through the opening between two leaning posts that gave a clear view of the porch and the three horses and the ground between. He pushed the barrel of the old Hotchkiss through the opening and settled flat to the earth and waited. The sun beat on his back and the stinging buffalo flies came and he did not move and patiently waited.

Inside the house the three men finished a final round of coffee with Clem Murphy and told him to remember they had been there most of the morning. They rinsed off their dishes in the tin dishpan and in straggling order started out the door.

Miley Bennett waited until they were past the porch in the open space going towards the horses. I do not know whether he saw them as wolves or as men or as anything at all except as evil moving scars on the decent bigness of the broad land. His first bullet smashed through the side of Jeff Clayton's head. The second tore a hole in the shoulder of one of the other two, going in clean and taking a piece of collarbone out with it and flattening him unconscious on the ground. The third kicked up dust beside the last of the three as he ducked behind the watering trough by the iron pump. The fourth crashed full into the breastbone of Clem Murphy as he ran through the doorway and on to the porch to see what was happening.

Silence dropped over the scene and the dust settled. Time passed and the sun beat down and the flies found the bodies. The man behind the watering trough saw a crack beneath it and through this studied every foot of the ground opposite him. The only cover was the stack of fence posts. At last he made out the dull deadliness of the gun barrel poking through. He waited and there was no movement. Revolver in hand, he peered cautiously over the top of the trough and fired four shots in quick aim at the small opening between the posts. He crouched low again and reloaded the revolver and waited and there was no movement and no sound.

His nerves became jumpy and he could no longer remain still. He leaped up and ran towards the horses, firing rapidly as he ran. He was on one and pulling it in a pawing semicircle when the bullet drilled into his back, snapping the bone and knocking him sidewise out of the saddle to hit a corral post and bounce in a broken heap to the ground.

⚬⫶⚬

Marshal Eakins found Miley Bennett late that afternoon. He found him in the little canyon. He was working doggedly with his small shovel, burying his sheep and marking the graves. He didn't seem surprised when Eakins rode up after ordering the posse to stay behind a ways. Only he couldn't seem to focus on anyone directly. He kept staring into space, and even while he was working he wasn't really focusing on it. He had nothing to say except to ask Eakins whether he could finish burying the sheep. When Eakins said no, there would have to be a trial before anything else could be done, he came along quietly, pulling back just long enough to tell the burro to take care of things while he was gone and keep the buzzards away and then letting them tie him on a horse and going along without any fuss, just staring at the bigness all around.

There was talk of a lynching in town, but not very strong because everyone respected Eakins and Federal Judge Stillwell was there on temporary circuit. I don't know what would have happened if the case had been in a State court. But Eakins said it was a Federal case because at bottom it was a controversy over Federal range and Judge Stillwell took jurisdiction.

No jury was needed because the plea was plain guilty. The trial took a little more than an hour, and Miley Bennett sat through it staring always out the window and hardly noticing what went on around him. All they got out of him beyond a few nods to direct questions was a single burst, after a question about Clem Murphy, that he didn't mean to shoot that one and just couldn't stop shooting and please couldn't they understand he didn't mean to shoot that one. The lawyer assigned to his defense argued extenuating circumstances fairly well, though his heart was not in it. Judge Stillwell cut the thing short by stating that the real extenuating circumstance was that the man had obviously lost his sanity. The Judge knew his audience and added that it was commonly known anyone who took to sheepherding was half-crazy to begin with and this made them all chuckle and held the grumbling down when he made the sentence life imprisonment. And Miley Bennett was staring out the window when they led him away to the jail where he would stay till they took him to the new Federal prison, and I knew it would take time but not too long before the whole meaning would sink home in him.

I guess that's all. Except perhaps the visit Marshal Eakins paid me the afternoon of the day they buried Miley Bennett with a powder-burned mouth and a mass of clotted blood where the back of his head had been. Eakins rode up to where I was stringing barbed wire. He didn't dismount. He simply reached down and handed me the gun.

"I reckon this is yours," he said.

"Yes," I said.

"Can't think of a charge," he said. "After all, you saved the Government the expense of feeding him for maybe a passel of years."

"I wasn't thinking of that," I said.

He nodded at me and reined the horse around and started back towards town. I watched him go, a man riding straight and steady across the big land.

Emmet Dutrow

Three days he was there on the rock ledge. I don't think he left it once. I couldn't be sure. I had things to do. But I could see him from my place and each time I looked he was there, a small dark-clad figure, immeasurably small against the cliff wall rising behind him.

Sometimes he was standing, head back and face up. Sometimes he was kneeling, head down and sunk into his shoulders. Sometimes he was sitting on one of the smaller stones.

Three days it was. And maybe the nights too. He was there when I went in at dusk and he was there when I came out in early morning. Once or twice I thought of going to him. But that would have accomplished nothing. I doubt whether he would even have noticed me. He was lost in an aloneness no one could penetrate. He was waiting for his God to get around to considering his case.

~:~

I guess this is another you'll have to let me tell in my own way. And the only way I know to tell it is in pieces, the way I saw it.

Emmet Dutrow was his name. He was of Dutch blood, at least predominantly so; the hard-shell deep-burning kind. He came from Pennsylvania, all the way to our new State of Wyoming with his heavy wide-bed wagon and slow, swinging yoke of oxen. He must have been months on the road, making his twelve to twenty miles a day when the weather was good and little or none when it was bad. The wagon carried food and farm tools and a few sparse pieces of stiff furniture beneath an old canvas. He walked and must have walked the whole way close by the heads of his oxen, guiding them with a leather thong fastened to the yoke. And behind about ten paces and to the side came his woman and his son Jess.

They camped that first night across the creek from my place. I saw him picketing the oxen for grazing and the son building a fire and the woman getting her pans from where they hung under the wagon's rear axle, and when my own chores were done and I was ready to go in for supper, I went to the creek and across on the stones in the shallows and towards their fire. He stepped out from it to confront me, blocking my way forward. He was a big man, big and broad and bulky, made more so by the queer clothes he wore. They were plain black of some rough thick material, plain black loose-fitting pants and plain black jacket like a frock-coat without any tails, and a plain black hat, shallow-crowned and stiff-brimmed. He had a square trimmed beard that covered most of his face, hiding the features, and eyes sunk far back so that you felt like peering close to see what might be in them.

Behind him the other two kept by the fire, the woman shapeless in a dark linsey-woolsey dress and pulled-forward shielding bonnet, the son dressed like his father except that he wore no hat.

I stopped. I couldn't have gone farther without walking right into him.

"Evening, stranger," I said.

"Good evening," he said. His voice was deep and rumbled in his throat with the self-conscious roll some preachers have in the pulpit. "Have you business with me?"

"There's a quarter of beef hanging in my springhouse," I said. "I thought maybe you'd appreciate some fresh meat."

"And the price?" he said.

"No price," I said. "I'm offering you some."

He stared at me. At least the shadow-holes where his eyes hid were aimed at me. "I'll be bounden to no man," he said.

The son had edged out from the fire to look at me. He waved an arm at my place across the creek. "Say mister," he said. "Are those cattle of yours—"

"Jess!" The father's voice rolled at him like a whip uncoiling. The son flinched at the sound and stepped back by the fire. The father turned his head again to me. "Have you any further business?"

"No," I said. I swung about and went back across the creek on the stones and up the easy slope to my little frame ranch house.

~:~

The next day he pegged his claim, about a third of a mile farther up the valley where it narrowed and the spring floods of centuries ago had swept around the curve above and washed the rock formation bare, leaving a high cliff to mark where they had turned. His quarter section spanned the space from the cliff to the present-day creek. It was a fair choice on first appearances; good bottom land, well-watered with a tributary stream wandering through, and there was a stand of cottonwoods back by the cliff. I had passed it up because I knew how the drifts would pile in below the cliff in winter. I was snug in the bend in the valley and the hills

63

behind protecting me. It was plain he didn't know this kind of country. He was right where the winds down the valley would hit him when the cold came dropping out of the mountains.

He was a hard worker and his son too. They were started on a cabin before the first morning was over, cutting and trimming logs and hauling them with the oxen. In two days they had the framework up and the walls shoulder high, and then the rain started and the wind, one of our late spring storms that carried a lingering chill and drenched everything open with a steady lashing beat. I thought of them there, up and across the creek, with no roof yet and unable to keep a fire going in such weather, and I pulled on boots and a slicker and an old hat and went out and waded across and went up to their place. It was nearly dark, but he and the son were still at work setting another log in place. They had taken pieces of the old canvas and cut holes for their heads and pulled the pieces down over their shoulders with their heads poking through. This made using their arms slow and awkward, but they were still working. He had run the wagon along one wall of the cabin, and with this covering one side and the rest of the old canvas fastened to hang down the other, it formed a low cave-like shelter. The woman was in there, sitting on branches for a floor, her head nearly bumping the bed of the wagon above. I could hear the inside drippings, different from the outside patter, as the rain beat through the cracks of the wagon planks and the chinks of the log wall.

He stepped forward again to confront me and stop me, a big bulgy shape in his piece of canvas topped by the beard and hat with the shadow-holes of the eyes between.

"It's a little wet," I said. "I thought maybe you'd like to come over to my place where it's warm and dry till this storm wears itself out. I can rig enough bunks."

"No," he said, rolling his tone with the organ stops out. "We shall do with what is ours."

I started to turn away and I saw the woman peering out at me from her pathetic shelter, her face pinched and damp under the bonnet, and I turned back.

"Man alive," I said, "forget your pride or whatever's eating you and think of your wife and the boy."

"I am thinking of them," he said. "And I am the shield that shall protect them."

I swung about and started away, and when I had taken a few steps his voice rolled after me. "Perhaps you should be thanked, neighbor. Perhaps you mean well."

"Yes," I said, "I did."

I kept on going and I did not look back and I waded across the creek and went up to my house and in and turned the lamp up bright and tossed a couple more logs into the fireplace.

I tried once more, about two weeks later. He had his cabin finished then, roofed with bark slabs over close-set poles and the walls chinked tight with mud from the creek bottom. He had begun breaking ground. His oxen were handy for that. They could do what no team of horses could do, could lean into the yoke and dig their split hooves into the sod and pull a heavy ploughshare ripping through the roots of our tough buffalo grass.

That seemed to me foolish, tearing up sod that was perfect for good cattle, getting ready for dirt farming way out there far from any markets. But he was doing it right. With the ground ploughed deep and the sod turned over, the roots would be exposed and would rot all through the summer and fall and by the next spring the ground would be ready to be worked and planted. And meanwhile he could string his fences and build whatever sheds he would need and get his whole place in shape.

We ought to be getting really acquainted, I thought, being the only neighbors there in the valley and more than that, for the nearest other place was two miles away towards town. It was up to me to make the moves. I was the first in the valley. He was the second, the new-comer.

As I said, I tried once more. It was a Saturday afternoon and I was getting ready to ride to town and see if there was any mail and pick up a few things and rub elbows with other folks a bit and I thought of them there across the creek, always working and penned close with only a yoke of oxen that couldn't make the eight miles in less than half a day each way. I harnessed the team to the buckboard and drove bouncing across the creek and to their place. The woman appeared in the cabin doorway, shading her eyes and staring at me. The son stopped ploughing off to the right and let go of the plough handles and started towards me. The father came around the side of the cabin and waved him back and came close to my wagon and stopped and planted his feet firmly and looked at me.

"I'm heading towards town," I said. "I thought maybe you'd like a ride in the back. You can look the place over and meet some of the folks around here."

"No, neighbor," he said. He looked at me and then let his voice out a notch. "Sin and temptation abide in towns. When we came past I saw the two saloons and a painted woman."

"Hell, man," I said, "you find those things everywhere. They don't bite if you let them alone."

"Ah, yes," he said. "Everywhere. All along the long way I saw them. They are everywhere. That is why I stopped moving at last. There is no escaping them in towns. Wherever people congregate, there is sin. I shall keep myself and mine apart."

"All right," I said. "So you don't like people. But how about your wife and the boy? Maybe they'd like a change once in a while."

His voice rolled out another notch. "They are in my keeping." He looked at me and the light was right and for the first time I saw his eyes, bright and hot in their shadow-holes. "Neighbor," he said, all stops out, "have I trespassed on your property?"

I swung the team in an arc and drove back across the creek. I unharnessed the team and sent them out in the side pasture with slaps on their rumps. I whistled the gray in and saddled him and headed for town at a good clip.

∼:∼

That was the last time. After that I simply watched what was happening up the valley. You could sum most of it with the one word—work. And the rest of it centered on the rock ledge at the base of the cliff where a hard layer jutted out about ten feet above the valley floor, flat on top like a big table. I saw him working there, swinging some tool, and after several days I saw what he was doing. He was cutting steps in the stone, chipping out steps to the ledge top. Then he took his son away from the ploughing for a day to help him heave and pry the fallen rocks off the ledge, all except three, a big squarish one and two smaller ones. Up against the big one he raised a cross made of two lengths of small log. Every day after that, if I was out early enough in the morning and late enough when the dusk was creeping in, I could see him and his woman and the son, all three of them on the ledge, kneeling, and I could imagine his voice rolling around them and echoing from the cliff behind them. And on Sundays, when there would be nothing else doing about their place at all, not even cooking smoke rising from the cabin chimney, they would be there hours on end, the woman and the son sometimes sitting on the two smaller stones, and the father, from his position leaning over the big stone, apparently reading from a book spread open before him.

It was on a Sunday, in the afternoon, that the son trespassed on my place. He came towards the house slow and hesitating like he was afraid something might jump and snap at him. I was sitting on the porch, the Winchester across my knees, enjoying the sunshine and waiting to see if the gopher that had been making holes in my side pasture would show its head. I watched him come, a healthy young figure in his dark pants and homespun shirt. When he was close, I raised my voice.

"Whoa, Jess," I said. "Aren't you afraid some evil might scrape off me and maybe get on you?"

He grinned kind of foolish and scrubbed one shoe-toe in the dirt. "Don't make fun of me," he said. "I don't hold with that stuff the way father does. He said I could come over anyway. He's decided perhaps you're all right."

"Thanks," I said. "Since I've passed the test, why not step up here and sit a spell?"

He did, and he looked all around very curious and after a while he said: "Father thought perhaps you could tell him what to do to complete the claim and get the papers on it."

I told him, and we sat awhile, and then he said: "What kind of a gun is that?"

"It's a Winchester," I said. "A repeater. A right handy weapon."

"Could I hold it once?" he said.

I slipped on the safety and passed it to him. He set it to his shoulder and squinted along the barrel, awkward and self-conscious.

"Ever had a gun of your own?" I said.

"No," he said. He handed the gun back quickly and stared at the porch floor. "I never had anything of my own. Everything belongs to father. He hasn't a gun anyway. Only an old shotgun and he won't let me touch it." And after a minute: "I never had even a nickel of my own to buy a thing with." And after a couple of minutes more: "Why does he have to be praying all the time, can you tell me that? That's all he ever does, working and praying. Asking forgiveness for sins. For my sins and Ma's sins too. What kind of sins have we ever had a chance to do? Can you tell me that?"

"No," I said. "No, I can't."

We sat awhile longer, and he was looking out at the pasture. "Say, are those cattle—"

"Yes," I said. "They're Herefords. Purebreds. Some of the first in these parts. That's why they're fenced tight."

"How'd you ever get them?" he said. "I mean them and everything you've got here."

"Well," I said, "I was a fool youngster blowing my money fast as I found it. Then one day I decided I didn't like riding herd on another man's cattle and bony longhorns at that when I knew there were better breeds. So, I started saving my pay."

"How long did it take?" he said.

"It was eleven years last month," I said, "that I started a bank account."

"That's a long time," he said. "That's an awful long time."

"How old are you, Jess?" I said.

"Nineteen," he said. "Nineteen four months back."

"When you're older," I said, "it won't seem like such a long time. When you're getting along some, time goes mighty fast."

"But I'm not older," he said.

"No," I said. "No. I guess you're not."

We sat awhile longer and then I got foolish. "Jess," I said, "the ploughing's done. That was the big job. The pressure ought to be letting up a bit now. Why don't you drop over here an afternoon or two and help me with my haying? I'll pay fair wages. Twenty-five cents an hour."

His face lit like a match striking. "Hey, mister!" Then: "But Father—"

"Jess," I said, "I never yet heard of work being sinful."

I wondered whether he would make it and Wednesday he did, coming early in the afternoon and sticking right with me till quitting hour. He was a good worker. He had to be to make up for the time he wasted asking me questions about the country and people roundabout, and my place and my stock and the years I'd spent in the saddle. He was back again on Friday. When I called quits and we went across the pasture to the house, the father was standing by the porch waiting.

"Good evening, neighbor," he said. "According to my son you mentioned several afternoons. They are done. I have come for the money."

"Dutrow," I said, "Jess did the work. Jess gets the money."

"You do not understand," he said, the tone beginning to roll. "My son is not yet of man's estate. Until he is I am responsible for him and the fruit of his labor is mine. I am sworn to guard him against evil. Money in an untried boy's pocket is a sore temptation to sin."

I went into the house and took three dollars from the purse in my jacket pocket and went out and to Jess and put them in his hand. He stood there with the hand in front of him, staring down at it.

"Jess! Come here!"

He came, flinching and unwilling, the hand still stiff in front of him, and the father took the money from it.

"I'm sorry, Jess," I said. "Looks like there'd be no point in your working here again."

He swung his eyes at me the way a whipped colt does and turned and went away, trying to hold to a steady walk and yet stumbling forward in his hurry.

"Dutrow," I said, "I hope that money burns your hand. You have already sinned with it."

"Neighbor," he said, "you take too much on yourself. My God alone shall judge my actions."

I went into the house and closed the door.

It was about a month later, in the middle of the week, that the father himself came to see me, alone and in mid-morning and wearing his black coat and strange black hat under the hot sun as he came to find me.

"Neighbor," he said, "have you seen my son this morning?"

"No," I said.

"Strange," he said. "He was not on his pallet when I rose. He missed morning prayers completely. He has not appeared at all."

He stood silent a moment. Then he raised an arm and pointed a thick forefinger at me. His voice rolled at its deepest. "Neighbor," he said, "if you have contrived with my son to go forth into the world, I shall call down the wrath of my God upon you."

"Neighbor Dutrow," I said, "I don't know what your son's doing. But I know what you're going to do. You're going to shut your yap and get the hell off my place."

I don't think he heard me. He wiped a hand across his face and down over his beard. "You must pardon me," he said. "I am sore overwrought with worry."

He strode away, down to the creek and left along it out of the valley towards town. The coat flapped over his hips as he walked and he grew smaller in the distance till he rounded the first hill and disappeared.

He returned in late afternoon, still alone and dusty and tired, walking slowly and staring at the ground ahead of him. He went past on the other side of the creek and to his place and stopped at the door of the cabin and the woman emerged and they went to the rock ledge and they were still kneeling there when the dark shut them out of my sight.

⁓⁚⁓

The next day, well into the afternoon, I heard a horse coming along the trace that was the beginning of the road into the valley and Marshal Eakins rode up to me by the barn and swung down awkward and stiff. He was tired and worn and his left shoulder was bandaged with some of the cloth showing through the open shirt collar.

"Afternoon, John," he said. "Any coffee in the pot you could warm over?"

In the house I stirred the stove and put the pot on to heat I pointed at his shoulder.

"One of our tough friends?" I said.

"Hell, no," he said. "I can handle them. This was an amateur. A crazy youngster."

When he had his cup, he took a first sip and leaned back in his chair.

"That the Dutrow place up the creek?" he said.

"Yes," I said.

"Must be nice neighbors," he said. "It was their boy drilled me." He tried the cup again and finished it in four gulps and reached for the pot. "His father was in town yesterday. Claimed the boy had run away. Right he was. The kid must have hid out during the day. Had himself a time at night. Pried a window at Walton's store. Packed himself a bag of food. Took a rifle and box of shells. Slipped over to the livery stable. Saddled a horse and lit out."

"He couldn't ride," I said.

"Reckon not," Eakins said. "Made a mess of the gear finding a bridle and getting it on. Left an easy track too. Didn't know how to make time on a horse. I took Patton and went after him. Must have had hours start, but we were tailing him before ten. Got off or fell off, don't know which, and scrambled into some rocks. I told him we had the horse and if he'd throw out the gun and come out himself there wouldn't be too much fuss about it. But he went crazy wild. Shouted something about sin catching up with him and started blazing away."

"He couldn't shoot," I said.

"Maybe not," Eakins said. "But he was pumping the gun as fast as he could and he got Patton dead center. We hadn't fired a shot."

Eakins started on the second cup.

"Well?" I said.

"So I went in and yanked him out," Eakins said. "Reckon I was a little rough. Patton was a good man."

He finished the second cup and set it down. "Got to tell his folks. Thought maybe you'd go along. Women give me the fidgets." He pushed at the cup with a finger. "Not much time. The town's a little hot. Trial will be tomorrow."

We walked down to the creek and across and up to their place. The woman appeared in the cabin doorway and stared at us. The father came from somewhere around the side of the cabin. He planted his feet firmly and confronted us. His head tilted high and his eyes were bright and hot in their shadow-holes. His voice rolled at us.

"You have found my son."

"Yes," Eakins said, "we've found him." He looked at me and back at the father and stiffened a little, and he told them, straight, factual. "The trial will be at ten tomorrow," he said. "They'll have a lawyer for him. It's out of my hands. It's up to the judge now."

And while he was talking, the father shrank right there before us. His head dropped and he seemed to dwindle inside his rough black clothes. His voice was scarcely more than a whisper.

"The sins of the fathers," he said, and was silent.

It was the woman who was speaking, out from the doorway and stretching up tall and pointing at him, the first and only words I ever heard her speak.

"You did it," she said. "You put the thoughts of sin in his head, always praying about it. And keeping him cooped in with never a thing he could call his own. On your head it is in the eyes of God. You drove him to it."

She stopped and stood still, looking at him, and her eyes were bright and hot and accusing in the pinched whiteness of her face, and she stood still looking at him.

They had forgotten we were there. Eakins started to speak again and thought better of it. He turned to me and I nodded and we went back along the creek and across and to the barn and he climbed stiffly on his horse and started towards town.

⌒:⌒

In the morning I saddled the gray and rode to the Dutrows' place. I was thinking of offering him the loan of the team and the buckboard. There was no sign of any activity at all. The place looked deserted. The cabin door was open and I poked my head in. The woman was sitting on a straight chair by the dead fireplace. Her hands were folded in her lap and her head was bowed over them. She was sitting still. There's no other way to describe what she was doing. She was just sitting.

"Where is he?" I said.

Her head moved in my direction and she looked vaguely at me and there was no expression on her face.

"Is he anywhere around?" I said.

Her head shook only enough for me to catch the slight movement and swung slowly back to its original position. I stepped back and took one more look around and mounted the gray and rode towards town, looking for him along the way, and did not see him.

I had no reason to hurry and when I reached the converted store building we used for a courthouse, it was fairly well crowded. Judge Cutler was on the bench. We had our own judge now for local cases. Cutler was a tall, spare man, full of experience and firm opinions, honest and independent in all his dealings with other people. That was why he was our judge. Marshal Eakins was acting as our sheriff until we would be better organized and have an office established. That was why he had taken charge the day before.

They brought in Jess Dutrow and put him in a chair at one side of the bench and set another at the other side for a witness stand. There was no jury because the plea was guilty. The lawyer they had assigned for Jess could do nothing except plead the youth of his client and the hard circumstances of his life. It did not take long, the brief series of witnesses to establish the facts. They called me to identify him and tell what I knew about him. They called Walton and the livery stable man to testify to the thefts. They called Eakins and had him repeat his story to put it in the court records. The defense lawyer was finishing his plea for a softening of sentence when there was a stirring in the room and one by one heads turned to stare at the outer doorway.

The father was there, filling the doorframe with his broad bulk in its black clothes. Dirt marks were on them as if he had literally wrestled with something on the ground. His hat was gone and his long hair flowed back unkempt. His beard was ragged and tangled and the cheeks above it were drawn as if he had not slept. But his voice rolled magnificently, searching into every corner of the room.

"Stop!" he said. "You are trying the wrong man!"

He came forward and stood in front of the bench, the wooden pedestal we used for a trial bench. He looked up at Judge Cutler on the small raised platform behind it.

"Mine is the guilt," he said. "On my head let the punishment fall. My son has not yet attained his twenty and first birthday. He is still of me and to me and I am responsible for aught that he does. He was put into my keeping by God, to protect him and guard him from temptation and bring him safely to man's estate. My will was not strong enough to control him. The fault therefore is in me, in his father that gave him the sins of the flesh and then failed him. On me the judgment I am here for it I call upon you to let him depart and sin no more."

Judge Cutler leaned forward. "Mr. Dutrow," he said in his precise, careful manner, "there is not a one of us here today does not feel for you. But the law is the law. We cannot go into the intangibles of human responsibilities you mention. Hereabout we hold that when a man reaches his eighteenth birthday he is a capable person, responsible for his own actions. Legally your son is not a minor. He must stand up to his own judgment."

The father towered in his dirty black coat. He raised an arm and swept it up full length. His voice fairly thundered.

"Beware, agent of man!" he said. "You would usurp the right of God Himself!"

Judge Cutler leaned forward a bit farther. His tone did not change. "Mr. Dutrow. You will watch quietly or I will have you removed from this room."

The father stood in the silence and dwindled again within his dark clothes. He turned slowly and looked over the whole room and everyone in it. Someone in the front row moved and left a vacant seat and he went to it and sat down, and his head dropped forward until his beard was spread over his chest.

"Jess Dutrow," Judge Cutler said, "stand up and take this straight. Have you anything to say for yourself?"

He stood up, shaky on his feet, then steadying. The whipped-colt look was a permanent part of him now. His voice cracked and climbed.

"Yes," he said. "I did it and he can't take that away from me! Everything's true and I don't give a damn! Why don't you get this over with?"

"Very well," Judge Cutler said. "There is no dispute as to the pertinent facts. Their logic is plain. You put yourself outside the law when you committed the thefts. While you were still outside the law you shot and killed a peace officer in the performance of his duty and wounded another. You did not do this by accident or in defense of your life. Insofar as the law can recognize, you did this by deliberate intent. By the authority vested in me as a legally sworn judge of the people of this State I sentence you to be hanged tomorrow morning at ten by this courthouse clock."

Most of us were not looking at Jess Dutrow. We were looking at the father. He sat motionless for a few seconds after Judge Cutler finished speaking. Then he roused in the chair and rose to his feet and walked steadily to the doorway and out, his head still low with the beard fanwise on his chest and his eyes lost and unseeable in their deep shadow-holes. I passed near him on the way home about an hour later and he was the same, walking steadily along, not slow, not fast, just steady and stubborn in his face. I called to him and he did not answer, did not even raise or turn his head.

∾:∽

The next morning I woke early. I lay quiet a moment trying to focus on what had wakened me. Then I heard it plain, the creaking of wagon wheels. I went to the door and looked out. In the brightening, pinkish light of dawn, I saw him going by on the other side of the creek. He had yoked the oxen to the big wagon and was pushing steadily along, leading them with the leather thong. I watched him going into the distance until I shivered in the chill morning air and I went back into the house and closed the door.

It was the middle of the afternoon when he returned, leading the oxen, and behind them on the wagon was the long rectangular box. I did not watch him. I simply looked towards his place every now and then. I had things to do and I was glad I had things to do.

I saw him stop the oxen by the cabin and go inside. Later I saw him standing outside the door, both arms thrust upward. I could not be sure, but I thought his head was moving and he was shouting at the sky. And later I saw him back in the shadow of the rock ledge digging the grave. And still later I saw him there digging the second grave.

·That brought me up short. I stared across the distance and there was no mistaking what he was doing. I set the pitchfork against the barn and went down to the creek and across on the stones and straight to him. I had to shout twice, close beside him, before he heard me.

He turned his head towards me and at last he saw me. His face above and beneath the beard was drawn, the flesh collapsed on the bones. He looked like a man riven by some terrible torment. But his voice was low. There was no roll in it. It was low and mild.

"Yes, neighbor?" he said.

"Damn it, man," I said, "what are you doing?"

"This is my wife," he said. His voice did not change, mild and matter-of-fact. "She killed herself." He drew a long breath and added gently, very gently: "With my butchering knife."

I stared at him and there was nothing I could say. At last: "I'll do what I can. I'll go into town and report it. You won't have to bother with that."

"If you wish," he said. "But that is all a foolishness. Man's justice is a mockery. But God's will prevail. He will give me time to finish this work. Then He will deal with me in His might."

He withdrew within himself and turned back to his digging. I tried to speak to him again and he did not hear me. I went to the cabin and looked through the doorway and went away quickly and to my place and saddled the gray and rode towards town. When I returned, the last shadows were merging into the dusk and the two graves were filled with two small wooden crosses by them and I saw him there on the ledge.

Three days he was there. And late in the night of the third day the rain began and the lightning streaked and the thunder rolled through the valley, and in the last hour before dawn I heard the deeper rolling rumble I had heard once before on a hunting trip when the whole face of a mountain moved and crashed irresistibly into a canyon below.

Standing on the porch in the first light of dawn, I saw the new broken outline of the cliff up and across the valley and the great slant jagged pile of stone and rubble below where the rock ledge had been.

We found him under the stones, lying crumpled and twisted near the big squarish rock with the wooden cross cracked and smashed beside him. What I remember is his face. The deep-sunk, sightless eyes were open and they and the whole face were peaceful. His God had not failed him. Out of the high heaven arching above had come the blast that gave him his judgment and his release.

General Pingley

T he Pingleys came into our section of Wyoming to take over the claim of a cousin who made the mistake of trying to drive a buckboard over a mountain trail while tipping a bottle of whisky. This cousin had proved up on the claim and the title was clear, and the Pingleys were the closest of kin. They were ready to leave their place in Nebraska for a middling good reason. From what I heard they had left other times from other places for the same reason, one that walked on two legs, an old man, Bert Pingley's father, old J. Clayburn Pingley.

They were a mixed lot, these Pingleys. Bert was a big mild middle-aged man, about the hardest-working and easiest-natured I've ever known. His wife was some years younger, a pretty woman, fluttery in her actions, and so shy that sometimes you might think she was silly in the head. There were two children, a little girl just beginning to walk and trying to hide in her mother's skirts when strangers were near, and a boy, coming seven or eight, I'd say, fair-sized for his age and easy-natured like his father. And, of course, there was the old man, stiff-backed as a ramrod, still fighting the Civil War thirty years after the last shot had been fired.

The first time I saw him he was wearing his old gray uniform coat and campaign hat. It was a Saturday afternoon, and I was in town to pick up any mail and rub elbows with other folks a bit. I saw him in Eiler's general store. He was ordering some tobacco and complaining about the price. He had a fringe of white chin whiskers that stood out straight when he talked.

"Double damn Yankees," he said. "Robbers. Every last one of you."

Eiler was surprised. He leaned forward on his counter. "Easy now, pop," he said. "I was born back in Georgia myself."

"A renegade, eh? Lived so long among these thieving Yankees you're the same."

I saw this big man, Bert, hurrying over, a smile busting his face wide open.

"Don't mind my father," he said. "It's one of his bad days. Can't seem to learn the war's over and forgotten." He smiled at Eiler and shrugged his shoulders a little. "You see, Father hasn't surrendered yet."

"You're double damned right I haven't. I'll keep right on telling every yellow-bellied bluecoat I find just what—"

Bert's smile stayed the same, but his hand on the old man's arm stopped the words. "Father, wait for me at the wagon. I'll bring your tobacco."

I saw him later the same afternoon in front of the old stage post where folks liked to meet and swap neighborhood news and wait for the mail coach. The three or four other men there with him must have been working on him because he was hopping mad when I came along. The chin whiskers were sticking out stiff as hog bristles.

"—never was a time," he was saying, "any Federal troops could stand to one of our charges. I mind me once when General Pickett—"

"Choke it, whiskers," said one of the men. "You rebs were licked before you started, only you didn't know it. Too many crazy old goats like you."

The old man pulled himself up even straighter. "Bert," he shouted, looking around. Right enough, Bert was hurrying over again, smiling again at the whole world. "Bert, you heard it. You're going to—"

"Shucks," said Bert. "You'd want I should smack him just because you riled him into calling names?"

"My own son! A coward in my own family!"

Bert's smile didn't change. That was when I began to like him. As I say, he was a big man. He could have taken any two of us there and my money would have been on him.

"Shucks, Father," he said. "You forget when we're needing supplies we come in under a truce flag."

The old man subsided like a sudden thunderstorm ending. "You're right, son. So we do." He took off his ancient campaign hat and bowed to the rest of us. "I'm sorry, gentlemen. I forgot myself. But perhaps some other time—" He marched off erect towards their wagon, and I saw it there, a white cotton handkerchief tied to a buggy whip whose butt was stuck between the sideboards.

Someone was standing close beside me. That was our marshal, Clyde Eakins. He was watching the old man.

"Stubborn old coot," I said.

"Yes," Eakins said. "But his kind of fun ain't exactly enjoyable after a while. Beginning already to get some folks' nerves ruffled."

He was not really so bad, not at first, anyway. You find some touchy ones anywhere you go. We had our share. But most of us were willing to let him talk his war. We couldn't be peeved at anyone who belonged to a man like Bert. I guess the old man had a right to a grudge at that. His other son, Bert's brother, had died at

Shiloh, and the shock of that, together with Federal troop occupation of the family place in Virginia, had killed his wife, Bert's mother. Then he lost everything he owned in the early carpetbag days. There was not much left for him except to tag along when Bert struck out into the new Territories.

For quite a while people in town tolerated his talk. They liked to stir him a little and watch the chin whiskers wag. They could count on Bert to step in smiling before real sparks flew. And they had a kind of admiration for the old man's unwavering belligerence. They began calling him the General, and he liked that. Bert didn't. "Shucks," Bert would say, "he wasn't a general. He was only a sort of reserve captain. Managed a supply depot down in North Carolina and didn't even hear a gun go off." Bert himself had. Plenty. He had fought through the four years, starting as a green kid of seventeen and coming out a man. But he never talked about that. It was a job he had to do, and when it was done it was finished. Maybe he felt that the old man did enough talking for the whole Pingley tribe.

It was in July that the town's temper turned. July Fourth. We always celebrated the day. A town committee would make the arrangements, and those like me who lived out a ways would be on hand to make a respectable crowd for the doings. There would be shooting matches, rifle and revolver, and things like that, and about mid-morning we would raise the flag on the town flagpole in the park space opposite the hotel and salute it with a lot of cheers and gunpowder. Then we would jam into the former storeroom we used for a courthouse and listen to the speechmaking and work up an appetite for the hot lunch some of the ladies always sold for the benefit of the volunteer fire department.

Judge Cutler usually made the main speech. He was dry and short with words on the bench, but his special orations were something to hear. This time he never got to finish. He was not much more than well unlimbered in the throat when someone standing by the door gave a shout and people turned to look where he was pointing, and there was a stampede through the doorway and across to the park space. Old J. Clayburn Pingley was standing stiff-backed by the pole. He had pulled down the flag and tossed it aside and run up an old Confederate flag instead.

People stopped in a half-circle around him and the pole gawking up at his faded old flag. And then things happened fast. Young Pard Wheeler, who had considerable celebrating under his belt, pulled his gun and aimed upwards and started shooting. I think he was only trying to cut the rope, but the bullets ripped through the flag and the rents showed plain. The old man screamed and started towards Wheeler, reaching in his side pocket and his hand came out with an old fashioned little derringer. Marshal Eakins scrambled quick and caught him and wrenched the arm, and the little weapon fell to the ground, and he broke loose from Eakins and went at Wheeler beating with his hands. Wheeler backed away trying to fend off the blows and stopped and gave the old man a push that sent him sprawling. And Bert Pingley burst out of the crowd and crashed a big fist to the side of Wheeler's head and Wheeler went down like a steer when you poleaxe it

Two things stick in my mind when I remember that. One is the look of the old man lying on the ground. He wasn't making any effort to get up. He was lying there, quiet now, leaning on one elbow and watching Bert, and mighty pleased about something. The other is the look of Bert Pingley standing there, big as the side of a mountain, not smiling, and disgusted with himself and ashamed.

Maybe I ought to add a third thing. Young Pard Wheeler, somehow acting for all of us, staggering a little when he got to his feet and trying to make Bert see that he understood what had happened.

The General wasn't amusing after that, not to most of the people around. I guess they remembered his scream and the little derringer coming out of his pocket. And there were some who were shocked at his hauling down the American flag. He wasn't a joke, a neighborhood character anymore. He was a nuisance that might cause trouble. But there wasn't any trouble because he was hardly ever in town again. That must have been Bert's doing. Bert was easy-natured. But he probably could be firm when he felt that he had to be.

The next I heard the old man was being sighted around the country, keeping out of people's way and getting about in a little buggy pulled by an old horse Bert let him use. Sometimes the boy would be with him and might wave a friendly arm, but the old man would drive right along, straight on the seat, not turning his head. He drove that buggy in the damndest places, where there were no roads and not even trails, smack across open range land and up into the mountains where you wouldn't think anything on wheels could go. When people spoke to Bert about it, Bert would just smile and shrug his shoulders. "Shucks," Bert would say, "he ain't worrying anybody, is he? Likes to camp out a few days at a time. Takes good care of the boy too." Then nobody was seeing much of him at all, and nobody seemed to know what he was doing, and Bert wasn't saying, even if he knew, and I was the first to find out what it was.

When the weather was right and no work pressing, I liked to saddle the gray and ride on up my valley and into the hills. After a few miles I'd be in the high country where the rock formations climbed and the bigness took you into itself in a comfortable quiet. Riding up there kept the horse in condition and my own mind too.

Sometime in late summer I was drifting along and came out on the wide chunk of tableland that was the far edge part of Sam Piegan's range. During dry periods when grass was sparse near his home spread, Piegan ran some of his cattle on those high plateaux. One year he had tried wintering some there and had built a line camp on this stretch of tableland. By spring he knew better, and was lucky to have enough of the cattle still alive to pay his man's wages. The only mark left was the abandoned log cabin. I had passed it a few times and noticed that the door was gone and the walls sagging and holes beginning to show in the roof.

When I saw it in the distance this time, it had a different look. Smoke was rising out of the stone chimney. I rode closer, and saw it had a makeshift door with pieces of old harness nailed for hinges and the walls were being chinked and new slabs of bark were on the roof. There was a pole sticking up from one corner, and flapping out from this was an old Confederate flag.

The door opened and the old man stood in the doorway. He had a battered Sharps carbine in his hands. "Ought to blast you out of that saddle," he said. "Yankee spy. Nosing around my fort."

"Easy, General," I said, "you're no bushwhacker. I didn't know you were here."

"You know it now. So, keep moving and don't come back." The chin whiskers stood out straight at me. "This is Confederate territory. By right of conquest." He waved the gun barrel to point at the cabin wall beside the door and I saw stretched there by its paws the skin of a good-sized black bear.

I sat on the gray chuckling. I couldn't help it. But I wasn't chuckling after a warning bullet from his carbine sang uncomfortably close by my right ear. I swung the gray and went into retreat, about as scared as mad. I never had any fondness for bullets moving in my direction. But half-way home, I was chuckling again. When I told Sam Piegan about it, he chuckled too. "The old boy can use the place all he wants. Maybe it'll keep him out of trouble. We'll pass the word around so nobody'll bother him."

~:~

I didn't ride out much the next months. Having knocked off the rest of the summer and fattening my three-year steers for market on special rations took the fall. But I saw him a few times driving past my place in his little buggy. The best route to that rebel roost of his was up my valley and left along the trail that climbed through the notch to the tablelands. Even that must have been a hard pull for his old horse. I didn't know how often he made the trip because sometimes I'd miss seeing him and only know he had gone past by chancing on his fresh wheel tracks in the mud where the road forded the valley stream not far from my house. Then the cold edge of late fall began to creep into the air and I didn't see him or his tracks at all.

Winter hit us early that year. It hit us weeks ahead of the usual first snow with a surprise storm that whipped over the near line of mountains and caught plenty of us unprepared. I know because it caught me and shook me for a nice loss. I liked to keep my market-age steers as long as possible, putting on the last possible pounds with good grain, and move them out just before the winter snows when the price was at a peak. I hadn't even begun thinking about moving them that year when the storm hit. I had checked my fences and filled the trays in the feedlot again and come in and gone to bed early, and along before midnight I woke startled and heard the wind shrieking in the chimney. I crawled out of the bunk and went to the door and opened it and the snow struck me in a sheet and stung my face. It was the worst kind, dry and fine and driving. I was plenty worried, not about the cattle themselves because I had stout shelters, but about what a real blizzard could mean. Not many hours of that kind of snow would choke the trails and even the travelled roads. If the cold held and later snows kept building the drifts, I might have to feed my steers all winter and sell in a dropping spring market.

I pulled on clothes and went out to take care of the horses. They were bunched under the roof-shelter out from the barn. I propped open the door to the stretch of stalls and didn't have to use any coaxing to get them in. There were knee-high drifts already by the time I pushed against the wind back to the house.

By morning I was snowed in tight, and the wind was still piling it down. I fought and floundered my way to the barn and saw the little path I made filling in fast again. I got one of the heavy work horses and climbed on him bareback and sent him ploughing back and forth from the barn to the house and return till I had a real path showing. But this kept on filling in, too, so I took fence posts from my stock pile and stuck them in the snow on the wind side of the path about six feet apart and found enough planks in the barn to set against them for the beginnings of a barrier. The snow packed against the planks and held them firm and the drifts started this way protected the path quite a bit. Snow kept blowing over the top and into the path, of course, but not so bad that I couldn't clear it away every few hours without too much trouble. I was set then for as long a siege as that storm wanted to give me. There was fodder in the barn and food in the house, and my woodpile would last a whole winter.

Along in the afternoon of that first day, the snow slackened and almost stopped, but the wind kept at its battering, and sometime during the night it whipped in reinforcements from far up in the mountains and began piling down the snow again. When it finally eased during the third day, my path was almost a tunnel, shoulder high on one side and a foot above my head on the other. If there had been a strong crust on the snow, I could have walked right on to the roof of the barn from the big drift along one side. I settled into a nice routine, catching up on my sleep, fussing around the barn and adjoining feedlot morning and evening, walking the horses along the path to take the stall-kinks out of their legs, and the rest of the time loafing snug and warm in the house. When I didn't remember about missing the market, I even enjoyed the quiet laziness.

It was late in the morning of the fifth or sixth day, I'm not sure now which, that I heard faint shouts outside. I went out on the porch, and there were two men bucking the drifts towards my house from where the road was under the snow. They were leading and almost dragging their horses by the reins. They were wrapped right for the weather with only a little of their faces showing, and I couldn't recognize them at first. They came closer, and I saw the big man in front was Bert Pingley and the one plodding behind was Marshal Eakins. They were beat, and no wonder. It was eight miles out from town to my place. They dropped the reins by the porch and nodded at me and went past me into the house and collapsed on the nearest chairs. I set a bottle on the table by Eakins and put the coffee pot to warming on the stove and went out again to their horses. I never knew two more grateful animals than those were when I led them to the barn and worked over them quick and pulled down some hay. They had plugged through drifts so long that their legs were quivering and could scarcely hold them up.

Back in the house I poured coffee around and waited for the others to talk. Bert gulped his cup and sat still, staring at the floor. Eakins finished his and poured himself another.

"Thanks, John," he said. "Nothing like coffee ever." He let the warmth work through him. He lifted an arm and pointed it on up the valley towards the hills, and let it drop. "The old man's up there," he said.

"Is he?" I said. "What the devil's he doing there?"

Bert raised his head briefly and let it drop again. "He had to get his flag."

"Yes," Eakins said. "Bert finally made it to town this morning for help and found me. The old fool left his flag up there and got to worrying about it. Started for it day before the storm. Must have been caught and couldn't get back."

I thought around that. "Well," I said, "I'd let the old coot hibernate there all winter. He's got shelter and firewood's handy."

"No," Eakins said. He shook his head and gulped his second cup of coffee and looked at me. "The boy's up there with him."

Bert raised his head again and almost shouted. "He had to get his flag, don't you see? His flag. And I couldn't go. Who knew about this storm anyway? It was his flag. Do you think I could say no?"

Eakins didn't pay any attention to him. Eakins just looked at me. "The boy's up there. They didn't take any supplies. Maybe a meal or two. We're coming back in the morning."

Eakins looked at me and I fidgeted on my chair. I felt the way you feel when there's something you know you have to do and don't want to do it.

"Hell, man," I said, "it can't be done. The notch will be plugged with drifts higher than this house."

Eakins just looked at me. "John," he said, "the old man's had his time. But the boy's up there. You know this country out here better'n about anyone else. Thought maybe you could figure a way through. An hour's rest and we'll start"

༄༅༌

I left them in the house and went to the barn and put out plenty of feed for the cattle and hay for the horses. I fastened the door open so the horses could go out all right if I was awhile getting home again. I passed by the gray and the big buckskin and the mare. She was with foal anyway. I looked over the work team and decided they were the ones. I didn't want speed or quickness or know-how. I wanted power and pull. I gave them a couple of quarts of grain each, and when they had eaten put on them the bridles with the long driving reins. I led them out by the porch and went in the house and wrapped myself good. I dropped the bottle in a side pocket and shook Eakins awake in his chair. I didn't need to shake Bert. He was up and had found my saddle-bags and was packing them with food. He strapped them together and went out and slung them over the back of one of the horses and Eakins and I followed him.

"We'll use the horses to break trail as far as we can," I said. "We'll alternate them in the lead. Then we'll be on our own."

I took the reins of one horse and started him down the track already broken towards the road and Bert followed with the other horse and Eakins tagged us. When we reached the road, I swung towards town, keeping to the track they had made coming out. I heard Bert shouting behind me and he sounded angry, and I kept straight on and I heard Eakins's voice. "Shut up and follow him." I held to the track till we cleared the entrance to my valley, and then swung sharp right across the open land and the untouched whiteness of the snow.

I had it all clear in my mind, the one way we might have a chance. I kept the lead, trying to stay out of the hollows where the snow was too deep for movement and to follow the rolling rises that the wind had swept fairly clear and work my way through the foothills to the right place in the rimrock where the mountains soared into their high climb. It was hard going almost every yard of the way. The snow was dry and loose and gave no real foothold, and there were times when there was nothing to do except plough ahead and try to smash through. More than once the horse fought forward till he was helpless, unable to strike down through the snow to the ground, and I had trouble getting him back out for a swing around to try another spot. After the first twenty minutes, he was dripping sweat and in about an hour he had enough.

I stopped and called back to Bert it was his turn and gave him the general direction and he took the lead with the other horse. He made a faster pace than I had, I guess because it was his boy and his father up there and not his horse fighting the drifts, and he was harsh urging it ahead. I thought of calling him on that, then thought better of it and kept my mouth shut. But I shouted time on him quicker than I had on myself. If we were going to kill my horses, we were going to do it the right way and conserve their strength and get the most out of them. We had a long way to go.

I don't know how many turns I called and alternated the horses. Time got to be hazy as we plugged along. Walking in that snow even with the trail broken by those big hooves wasn't easy. And for the last couple of hours we were moving uphill most of the time I know the horses were done, completely exhausted, with the strength out of them, when we hit the steep rocky slope, almost a cliff, I was looking for. I didn't dare tell Bert where we would head next or he would have started right on. I let him stew while I scraped the thick sweat out of the horses' matted hair and tied them under the shelter of an overhanging ledge and yanked down some pine branches for them.

"All right," I said when I was ready. "It's not far now. If we can scramble up here, we'll come out on those flat stretches. They're like steps up the mountain. Third one up's the place."

I was right that this was where we could make it. That rocky slope was almost bare of snow except where out-cropping ledges had caught it. We could zigzag up where the footholds were best and pull ourselves along by grabbing at the big rocks. Climbing took the breath out of us, but the flat stretches themselves were the really hard going. They had their own drifts and we had to break our own trail. I doubt whether Eakins and I could have crossed them without Bert smashing ahead of us. We were at the bottom of the last slope when we heard a shot somewhere above us. We shouted, but our voices would not carry, and then we couldn't shout because we needed all our breath for the final scramble to the top.

~:~

I wonder sometimes what exactly we expected to see when we reached the top. Not the peaceful scene we found. Everything was quiet and lovely in the late afternoon light. For some reason the quietness and the loveliness remain in my mind. All the long way we had been too busy fighting the snow to appreciate what was around us. Now it hit me suddenly. The cabin off in the distance, small and alone against the mountain wall behind it, was serene and untroubled in the midst of the white wonder and smoke was rising from its chimney. Close to us, where the wagon trail swung in an arc, was the little buggy, the wheels buried in a drift, and we could see the track it had made from the cabin and the spread snow where the horse had floundered and been caught and had been unharnessed and led back towards the cabin. And perched on the buggy seat was the boy, alive and alert and staring at us with the battered Sharps carbine across his knees.

Eakins was the first to speak. "What was that shot?" he said.

The boy gulped and found his voice. "Grandpa told me to shoot every so often, so somebody might hear. You took an awful long time. I've only got two bullets left." He stared at us, and suddenly he dropped the gun clattering on the buggy floorboards and jumped down and struggled through the snow towards us, and Bert leaped with long strides to meet him and gather him up, and the boy was crying and laughing in his arms and saying, "I knew you'd come." And after a moment he quieted and looked at Eakins and me. "Grandpa said some of you'd come too. He said even if you are Yankees, you'd worry about us and come get us."

Bert jerked his head towards the cabin. "Is he all right?"

"Oh, sure he is. I've kept the fire going like he said." Suddenly the boy was very serious. "He's broke his leg, though. But he says that isn't bad. He chopped and chopped an awful lot of wood and then he fell on something and his leg broke. But he says that'll get all right. He says he has good bones."

We started towards the cabin, Bert carrying the boy, and when we were almost there the boy was serious again.

"Please be quiet," he said. "Grandpa's awful tired and sleeps a lot. He hasn't waked up at all yet today."

We went in quietly, and when we saw the stillness of the thin old figure on the bunk, we knew that he would never waken. I saw Bert's face set in stern lines, and he put the boy down gently and went over and stood staring at the still figure. Eakins took the boy by an arm and led him outside, and I followed.

"Is daddy going to wake him?" the boy said.

"No," Eakins said. "Not right now." He looked off into the distance and then at the boy again. "You hungry?"

"No," the boy said. "I don't think so. My stomach feels kind of puffy. We've only had a bag of dried apples that was here, and I only eat a little bowlful at a time and only twice a day the way grandpa says. But dried apples make your stomach feel puffy."

Eakins looked off into the distance again, into the wide vast openness where the slope dropped away as if it were the edge of the world. "Your grandfather," he said, "has he been eating them too?"

"Oh, no," the boy said. "He doesn't want any. He says dried apples are bad for anyone with a broken leg."

I saw Bert in the doorway and Eakins did too and spoke quickly to him. "Take the boy, Bert, and backtrack to where we left the horses. Get a fire going and rustle out some food. Start him in easy on it. John and I'll take care of things here."

~:~

We stood by the bunk and looked down at the wasted figure, at the thin old face with its sunken cheeks and pathetic fringe of chin whiskers.

"He was a stubborn old coot," I said.

"Yes," Eakins said, "he was."

I pulled the blanket up over the face, and together we made the best temporary grave we could to hold him till spring and proper burial in town. We scraped away snow and used the axe to dig into the hard ground. We yanked down part of the chimney to pile rocks over the grave so no animal could get at him. And just before we left, Eakins went inside again and came out with the torn flag and tied it to the pole from the corner of the cabin and struck the pole firmly in among the rocks.

The last thing I saw in the fading light, as we went over the edge of the tableland and started down the steep slope, was that old flag whipping out straight and stiff in the mountain wind.

PART TWO

Sergeant Houck

Sergeant Houck stopped his horse just below the top of the ridge ahead. The upper part of his body was silhouetted against the skyline as he rose in his stirrups to peer over the crest. He urged the horse on up and the two of them, the man and the horse were sharp and distinct against the copper sky. After a moment he turned and rode down to the small troop waiting. He reined beside Lieutenant Imler.

"It's there, sir. Alongside a creek in the next hollow. Maybe a third of a mile."

Lieutenant Imler regarded him coldly. "You took your time, Sergeant. Smack on the top too."

"Couldn't see plain, sir. Sun was in my eyes."

"Wanted them to spot you, eh, Sergeant?"

"No, sir. Sun was bothering me. I don't think—"

"Forget it, Sergeant. I don't like this either."

Lieutenant Imler was in no hurry. He led the troop slowly up the hill. He waited until the men were spread in a reasonably straight line just below the ridge top. He sighed softly to himself. The real fuss was fifty-some miles away. Captain McKay was hogging the honors there. Here he was tied to this disgusting sideline detail. Twenty men. Ten would have been enough. Ten, and an old hand like Sergeant Houck with no officer to curb his style. Thank the War Department for sergeants, the pickled-in-salt variety. They could do what no commissioned officer could do. They could forget orders and follow their own thoughts and show themselves on the top of a hill.

Lieutenant Imler sighed again. Even Sergeant Houck must think this had been time enough. He lifted his drawn sabre. "All right, men. If we had a bugler, he'd be snorting air into it right now."

Sabre pointing forward, Lieutenant Imler led the charge up and over the crest and down the long slope to the Indian village. There were some scattered shots from bushes by the creek, ragged pops indicating poor powder and poorer weapons, probably fired by the last of the old men left behind when the young braves departed in war paint ten days before. A few of the squaws and children, their dogs tagging, could still be seen running into the brush. They reached cover and faded from sight, disappeared into the surrounding emptiness. The village was silent and deserted and dust settled in the afternoon sun.

Lieutenant Imler surveyed the ground taken. "Spectacular achievement," he muttered to himself. He beckoned Sergeant Houck to him.

"Your redskin friend was right, Sergeant. This is it."

"Knew he could be trusted, sir."

"Our orders are to destroy the village. Send a squad out to round up any stock. There might be some horses around. We're to take them in." Lieutenant Imler waved an arm at the thirty-odd skin-and-pole huts. "Set the others to pulling those down. Burn what you can and smash everything else."

"Right, sir."

Lieutenant Imler rode into the slight shade of the cottonwoods along the creek. He wiped the dust from his face and set his campaign hat at a fresh angle to ease the crease made by the band on his forehead. Here he was, hot and tired and way out at the end of nowhere with another long ride ahead, while Captain McKay was having it out at last with Gray Otter and his renegade warriors somewhere between the Turkey Foot and the Washakie. He relaxed to wait in the saddle, beginning to frame his report in his mind.

"Pardon, sir."

Lieutenant Imler swung in the saddle to look around. Sergeant Houck was afoot, was standing near with something in his arms, something that squirmed and seemed to have dozens of legs and arms.

"What the devil is that, Sergeant?"

"A baby, sir. Or rather, a boy. Two years old, sir."

"How the devil do you know? By his teeth?"

"His mother told me, sir."

"His mother?"

"Certainly, sir. She's right here."

Lieutenant Imler saw her then, close to a neighboring tree, partially behind the trunk, shrinking into the shadow and staring at Sergeant Houck and his squirming burden. He leaned to look closer. She was not young. She might have been any age in the middle years. She was shapeless in the sack-like skin covering with slit-holes for her arms and head. She was sun- and windburned dark, yet not as dark as he expected. And there was no mistaking her hair. It was light brown and long and braided, and the braid was coiled around on her head.

"Sergeant! It's a white woman!"

"Right, sir. Her name's Cora Sutliff. The wagon train she was with was wiped out by a raiding party. She and another woman were taken along. The other woman died. She didn't. The village here bought her. She's been in Gray Otter's lodge." Sergeant Houck smacked the squirming boy briskly and tucked him under one arm. He looked straight at Lieutenant Imler. "That was three years ago, sir."

"Three years? Then that boy—"

"That's right, sir."

~:~

Captain McKay looked up from his desk to see Sergeant Houck stiff at attention before him. It always gave him a feeling of satisfaction to see this big slab of cross-grained granite that Nature had hewed into the shape of a man. The replacements they were sending these days, raw and unseasoned, were enough to shake his faith in the Service. But as long as there remained a sprinkling of these case-hardened old-time regulars, the Army would still be the Army.

"At ease, Sergeant."

"Thank you, sir."

Captain McKay drummed his fingers on the desk. This was a ridiculous proposition. There was something incongruous about it and the solid, impassive bulk of Sergeant Houck made it seem even more so.

"That woman, Sergeant. She's married. The husband's alive, wasn't with the train when it was attacked. He's been located, has a place about twenty miles out of Laramie. The name's right and everything checks. You're to take her there and turn her over with the troop's compliments."

"Me, sir?"

"She asked for you. The big man who found her. Lieutenant Imler says that's you."

Sergeant Houck considered this behind the rock mask of weather-carved face. "And about the boy, sir?"

"He goes with her." Captain McKay drummed on the desk again. "Speaking frankly, Sergeant, I think she's making a mistake. I suggested she let us see the boy got back to the tribe. Gray Otter's dead, and after that affair two weeks ago there's not many of the men left. But they'll be on the reservation now and he'd be taken care of. She wouldn't hear of it, said if he had to go she would too." Captain McKay felt his former indignation rising again. "I say she's playing the fool. You agree with me, of course."

"No, sir. I don't."

"And why the devil not?"

"He's her son, sir."

"But he's—Well, that's neither here nor there, Sergeant. It's not our affair. We deliver her and there's an end to it. You'll draw expense money and start within the hour. If you push along, you can make the stage at the settlement. Two days going and two coming. That makes four. If you stretch it another coming back, I'll be too busy to notice. If you stretch it past that, I'll have your stripes. That's all."

"Right, sir." Sergeant Houck straightened and swung about and started for the door.

"Houck."

"Yes, sir."

"Take good care of her—and that damn kid."

"Right, sir."

❦

Captain McKay stood by the window and watched the small cavalcade go past towards the post gateway. Lucky that his wife had come with him, even on this last assignment to this God-forsaken station lost in the prairie wasteland. Without her they would have been in a fix with the woman. As it was, the woman looked like a woman now. And why shouldn't she, wearing his wife's third-best, crinoline dress? It was a bit large, but it gave her a proper feminine appearance. His wife had enjoyed fitting her, from the skin out, everything except shoes. Those were too small. The woman seemed to prefer her worn moccasins anyway. And she was uncomfortable in the clothes. But she was decently grateful for them, insisting she would have them returned or would pay for them somehow. She was riding past the window, side-saddle on his wife's horse, still with that strange shrinking air about her, not so much frightened as remote, as if she could not quite connect with what was happening to her, what was going on around her.

Behind her was Private Lakin, neat and spruce in his uniform, with the boy in front of him on the horse. The boy's legs stuck out on each side of the small improvised pillow tied to the forward arch of the saddle to give him a better seat. He looked like a weird, black-haired doll bobbing with the movements of the horse.

And there beside the woman, shadowing her in the midmorning sun, was that extra incongruous touch, the great granite hulk of Sergeant Houck, straight in his saddle with the military erectness that was so much a part of him that it would never leave him, solid, impassive, taking this as he took everything, with no excitement and no show of any emotion, a job to be done.

They went past, and Captain McKay watched them ride out through the gateway. It was not quite so incongruous after all. As he had discovered on many a tight occasion, there was something comforting in the presence of that big, angular slab of a man. Nothing ever shook him. He had a knack of knowing what needed to be done whatever the shifting circumstances. You might never know exactly what went on inside his close-cropped, hard-pan skull, but you could be certain that what needed to be done he would do.

Captain McKay turned back to his desk. He would wait for the report, terse and almost illegible in crabbed handwriting, but he could write off this detail as of this moment. Sergeant Houck had it in hand.

~:~

They were scarcely out of sight of the post when the boy began his squirming. Private Lakin clamped him to the pillow with a capable right hand. The squirming persisted. The boy seemed determined to escape from what he regarded as an alien captor. Silent, intent, he writhed on the pillow. Private Lakin's hand and arm grew weary. He tickled his horse forward with his heels until he was close behind the others.

"Beg pardon."

Sergeant Houck shifted in his saddle and looked around. "Yes?"

"He's trying to get away. It'd be easier if I tied him down. Could I use my belt?"

Sergeant Houck held in his horse to drop back alongside Private Lakin. "Kids don't need tying," he said. He reached out and plucked the boy from in front of Private Lakin and laid him, face down, across the withers of his own horse and smacked him sharply. He picked the boy up again and reached out and set him again on the pillow. The boy sat still, very still, making no movement except that caused by the sliding motion of the horse's foreshoulders. Sergeant Houck pushed his left hand into his left side pocket and it came forth with a fistful of small hard biscuits.

He passed these to Private Lakin. "Stick one of these in his mouth when he gets restless."

Sergeant Houck urged his horse forward until he was beside the woman once more. She had turned her head to watch, and she stared sidewise at him for a long moment, then looked straight forward again along the wagon trace before them.

They came to the settlement in the same order, the woman and Sergeant Houck side by side in the lead, Private Lakin and the boy tagging at a respectful distance. Sergeant Houck dismounted and helped the woman down and plucked the boy from the pillow and handed him to the woman. He unfastened one rein from his horse's bridle and knotted it to the other, making them into a lead strap. He did the same to the reins of the woman's horse. He noted Private Lakin looking wistfully at the painted front of the settlement's one saloon and tapped him on one knee and handed him the ends of the two straps. "Scat," he said, and watched Private Lakin turn his horse and ride off leading the other two horses. He took the boy from the woman and tucked him under one arm and led the way into the squat frame building that served as general store and post office and stage stop. He settled the woman on a preserved-goods box and set the boy in her lap and went to the counter to arrange for their fares. When he returned to sit on another box near her, the entire permanent male population of the settlement had assembled just inside the door, all eleven of them staring at the woman.

"... that's the one ..."

"... an Indian had her ..."

"... shows in the kid ..."

Sergeant Houck looked at the woman. She was staring at the floor. The blood was retreating from beneath the skin of her face, making it appear old and leathery. He started to rise and felt her hand on his arm. She had leaned over quickly and clutched his sleeve.

"Please," she said. "Don't make trouble on account of me."

"Trouble?" said Sergeant Houck. "No trouble." He rose and confronted the fidgeting men by the door. "I've seen kids around this place. Some of them small. This one now needs decent clothes and the store here doesn't stock them."

The men stared at him, startled, and then at the wide-eyed boy in his clean but patched skimpy cloth covering. Five or six of them went out through the door and disappeared in various directions. The others scattered through the store, finding little businesses to excuse their presence. Sergeant Houck stood sentinel, relaxed and quiet, by his box, and those who had gone out straggled back, several embarrassed and empty-handed, the rest proud with their offerings.

Sergeant Houck took the boy from the woman's lap and stood him on his box. He measured the offerings against the small body and chose a small red flannel shirt and a small pair of faded overalls. He peeled the boy with one quick motion, ripping away the old cloth, and put the shirt and overalls on him. He set the one pair of small scuffed shoes aside. "Kids don't need shoes," he said. "Only in winter." He heard the sound of hooves and stepped to the door to watch the stage approach and creak to a stop, the wheels sliding in the dust. He looked back to see the men inspecting the boy to that small individual's evident satisfaction and urging their other offerings upon the woman. He strode among them and scooped the boy under one arm and beckoned the woman to follow and went out the door to the waiting old Concord coach. He deposited the boy on the rear seat inside and turned to watch the woman come out of the store escorted by the male population of the settlement. He helped her into the coach and nodded up at the driver on his high box seat and swung himself in. The rear seat groaned and sagged as he sank into it beside the woman with the boy between them. The woman peered out the window by her, and suddenly, in a shrinking, experimental gesture, she waved at the men outside. The driver's whip cracked and the horses lunged into the harness and the coach rolled forward, and a faint suggestion of warm color showed through the tan of the woman's cheeks.

~:~

They had the coach to themselves for the first hours. Dust drifted steadily through the windows and the silence inside was a persistent thing. The woman did not want to talk. She had lost all liking for it and would speak only when necessary, and there was no need. And Sergeant Houck used words with a natural and unswerving economy, for the sole simple purpose of conveying or obtaining information that he regarded as pertinent to the business immediately in hand. Only once did he speak during these hours and then only to set a fact straight in his mind. He kept his eyes fixed on the dusty scenery outside as he spoke.

"Did he treat you all right?"

The woman made no pretense of misunderstanding him. Her thoughts leaped back and came forward through three years and she pushed straight to the point with the single word. "Yes," she said.

The coach rolled on and the dust drifted. "He beat me once," she said, and the coach rolled on, and four full minutes passed before she finished this in her own mind and in the words: "Maybe it was right. I wouldn't work."

Sergeant Houck nodded. He put his right hand in his right

pocket and fumbled there to find one of the short straight straws and bring it forth. He put one end of this in his mouth and chewed slowly on it and watched the dust whirls drift past.

They stopped for a quick meal at a lonely ranch-house and ate in silence while the man there helped the driver change horses. Then the coach rolled forward and the sun began to drop overhead. It was two mail stops later, at the next change, that another passenger climbed in and plopped his battered suitcase and himself on the front seat opposite them. He was of medium height and plump. He wore city clothes and had quick eyes and features small in the plumpness of his face. He took out a handkerchief and wiped his face and removed his hat to wipe all the way up his forehead. He laid the hat on top of the suitcase and moved restlessly on the seat, trying to find a comfortable position. His movements were quick and nervous. There was no quietness in him.

"You three together?"

"Yes," said Sergeant Houck.

"Your wife, then?"

"No," said Sergeant Houck. He looked out the window on his side and studied the far horizon. The coach rolled on, and the man's quick eyes examined the three of them and came to brief rest on the woman's feet.

"Begging your pardon, lady, but why do you wear those things? Moccasins, aren't they? They more comfortable?"

She looked at him and down again at the floor and shrank back farther in the seat and the blood began to retreat from her face.

"No offense, lady," said the man. "I just wondered—" He stopped. Sergeant Houck was looking at him.

"Dust's bad," said Sergeant Houck. "And the flies this time of year. Best to keep your mouth closed."

He looked again out the window and the coach rolled on, and the only sounds were the running beat of the hooves and the creakings of the old coach.

A front wheel struck a stone and the coach jolted up at an angle and lurched sideways and the boy gave a small whimper. The woman pulled him to her and on to her lap.

"Say," said the man, "where'd you ever pick up that kid? Looks like—" He stopped.

Sergeant Houck was reaching up and rapping a rock fist against the top of the coach. The driver's voice could be heard shouting at the horses and the coach slowed and the brakes bit on the wheels and the coach stopped. One of the doors opened and the driver peered in. Instinctively he picked Sergeant Houck.

"What's the trouble, soldier?"

"No trouble," said Sergeant Houck. "Our friend here wants to ride up on the box with you." He looked at the plump man. "Less dust up there. It's healthy and gives a good view."

"Now, wait a minute," said the man. "Where'd you get the idea—"

"Healthy," said Sergeant Houck.

The driver looked at the bleak, impassive hardness of Sergeant Houck and at the twitching softness of the plump man. "Reckon it would be," he said. "Come along. I'll boost you up."

The coach rolled forward and the dust drifted and the miles went under the wheels. They rolled along the false-fronted one street of a mushroom town and stopped before a frame building tagged "Hotel." One of the coach doors opened and the plump man retrieved his hat and suitcase and scuttled away and across the porch and into the building. The driver appeared at the coach door. "Last meal here before the night run," he said, and wandered off around the building. Sergeant Houck stepped to the ground and helped the woman out and reached back in and scooped up the boy, tucked him under an arm, and led the way into the building.

When they came out, the shadows were long and fresh horses had been harnessed and a bent, footsore old man was applying grease to the axles. When they were settled again on the rear seat, two men emerged from the building lugging a small but heavy chest and hoisted it into the compartment under the high driving seat. Another man, wearing a close-buttoned suitcoat and curled-brim hat and carrying a shotgun in the crook of one elbow, ambled into sight around the corner of the building and climbed to the high seat. A moment later a new driver, whip in hand, followed and joined him on the seat and gathered the reins into his left hand. The whip cracked and the coach lurched forward and a young man ran out of the low building across the street carrying a saddle by the two stirrup straps swinging and bouncing against his thigh. He ran alongside and heaved the saddle up to fall thumping on the roof inside the guardrail. He pulled at the door and managed to scramble in as the coach picked up speed. He dropped on to the front seat, puffing deeply.

"Evening, ma'am," he said between puffs. "And you, General." He leaned forward to slap the boy gently along the jaw. "And you too, bub."

Sergeant Houck looked at the lean length of the young man, at the faded levis tucked into short high-heeled boots, the plaid shirt, the brown handkerchief knotted around the tanned neck, the amiable, competent young face. He grunted a greeting, unintelligible but a pleasant sound.

"A man's legs ain't made for running," said the young man. "Just to fork a horse. That last drink was near too long."

"The Army'd put some starch in those legs," said Sergeant Houck.

"Maybe. Maybe that's why I ain't in the Army." The young man sat quietly, relaxed to the jolting of the coach. "Is there some other topic of genteel conversation you folks'd want to worry some?"

"No," said Sergeant Houck.

"Then maybe you'll pardon me," said the young man. "I hoofed it a lot of miles today." He worked hard at his boots and at last got them off and tucked them out of the way on the floor. He hitched himself up and over on the seat until he was resting on one hip. He put an arm on the window sill and cradled his head on it. His eyes closed. They opened and his head rose a few inches. "If I start sliding, just raise a foot and give me a shove." His head dropped down and the dust whirls outside melted into the dusk and he was asleep.

Sergeant Houck felt a small bump on his left side. The boy had toppled against him and was struggling back to sitting position, fighting silently to defeat the drowsiness overcoming him. Sergeant Houck scooped him up and set the small body across his lap with the head nestled into the crook of his right arm. He leaned his head down and heard the soft little last sigh as the drowsiness won. The coach rolled on, and he looked out into the dropping darkness and saw the deeper black of hills far off on the horizon. He looked sidewise at the woman and dimly made out the outline of her head falling forward and jerking back up, and he reached his left arm along the top of the seat until the hand touched her far shoulder. Faintly he saw her eyes staring at him and felt her shoulder stiffen and then relax as she moved closer and leaned towards him. He slipped down lower in the seat so that her head could reach his shoulder and he felt the gentle touch of the topmost strands of the braided coil of brown hair on his neck above his shirt collar. He waited patiently, and at last he could tell by her steady deep breathing that all fright had left her and all her thoughts were stilled.

The coach rolled on and reached a rutted stretch and began to sway and the young man stirred and began to slide on the smooth leather of his seat. Sergeant Houck put up a foot and braced it against the seat edge and the young man's body came to rest against it and was still. Sergeant Houck leaned his head back on the top of the seat and against the wall of the coach. The stars emerged in the clear sky and the coach rolled on, and the running beat of the hooves had the rhythm of a cavalry squad at a steady trot and gradually the great granite slab of Sergeant Houck softened slightly into sleep.

～:～

Sergeant Houck awoke as always all at once and aware. The coach had stopped. From the sounds outside fresh horses were being buckled into the traces. The first light of dawn was creeping into the coach. He raised his head and the bones of his neck cracked and he realized that he was stiff in various places, not only his neck but his right arm where the sleeping boy still nestled and his leg stretched out with the foot braced against the opposite seat.

The young man there was awake. He was still sprawled along the hard leather cushion, but he was pulled back from the braced foot and his eyes were open. He was inspecting the vast leather sole of Sergeant Houck's boot. His eyes flicked up and met Sergeant Houck's eyes, and he grinned.

"That's impressive footwear," he whispered. "You'd need starch in the legs with hooves like that." He sat up and stretched, long and reaching, like a lazy young animal. "Hell," he whispered again, "you must be stiff as a branding iron."

He took hold of Sergeant Houck's leg at the knee and hoisted it slightly so that Sergeant Houck could bend it and ease the foot down to the floor without disturbing the sleeping woman leaning against him. He stretched out both hands and gently lifted the sleeping boy from Sergeant Houck's lap and sat back with the boy in his arms.

Sergeant Houck began closing and unclosing his right hand to stimulate the blood circulation in the arm. The coach rolled forward and the first copper streak of sunlight found it and followed it.

The young man studied the boy's face. "Can't be yours," he whispered.

"No," whispered Sergeant Houck.

"Must have some Indian strain."

"Yes."

The young man whispered down at the sleeping boy. "You can't help that, can you, bub?"

"No," said Sergeant Houck suddenly, full voice, "he can't."

The woman jerked upright and pulled over to the window on her side, rubbing at her eyes. The boy awoke, wide awake on the instant, and saw the unfamiliar face above him and began to squirm violently.

The young man clamped his arms tighter. "Morning, ma'am," he said. "Looks like I ain't such a good nursemaid."

Sergeant Houck reached one hand and plucked up the boy by a grip on the small overalls and deposited him in sitting position on the seat beside the young man. The boy stared at Sergeant Houck and sat still, very still.

The sun climbed into plain view and the coach rolled on. It was stirring the dust of a well-worn road now. It stopped where another crossed and the driver jumped down to deposit a little packet of mail in a box on a short post

The young man inside pulled on his boots. He bobbed his head in the direction of a group of low buildings up the side road.

"Think I'll try it there. They'll be peeling broncs about now and the foreman knows I can sit a saddle." He opened a door and jumped to the ground and whirled to poke his head in. "Hope you make it right," he said, "wherever you're heading."

The door closed and he could be heard scrambling up the back of the coach to get his saddle. There was a thump as he and the saddle hit the ground and then voices began outside, rising in tone.

Sergeant Houck pushed his head through the window beside him. The young man and the driver were facing each other over the saddle. The young man was pulling the pockets of his levis inside out.

"Lookahere, Will," he said, "you can see they're empty. You know I'll kick in soon as I have some cash. Hell, I've hooked rides with you before."

"Not now no more," said the driver. "The company's sore. They hear of this they'd have my job. I'll have to hold the saddle."

The young man's voice had a sudden bite. "You touch that saddle and they'll pick you up in pieces from here to breakfast."

Sergeant Houck fumbled for his inside jacket pocket. This was difficult with his head through the window, but he succeeded in finding it. He whistled sharply. The two men swung to see him. His eyes drilled at the young man. "There's something on the seat in here. Must have slipped out of your pocket." He saw the young man stare, puzzled, and start towards the door. He pulled his head back and was sitting quietly in place when the door opened.

The young man leaned in and saw the two silver dollars on the hard seat and swivelled his head to look up at Sergeant Houck. Anger blazed in his eyes and he looked at the impassive rock of Sergeant Houck"s face and the anger faded.

"You've been in spots yourself," he said.

"Yes," said Sergeant Houck.

"And maybe were helped out of them."

"When I was a young squirt with more energy than brains," said Sergeant Houck. "Yes."

The young man grinned. He picked up the two coins in one hand and swung the other to slap Sergeant Houck's leg, sharp and stinging and grateful. "Age ain't hurting you any, General," he said, and closed the door.

The coach rolled on, and the woman looked at Sergeant Houck and the minutes passed and still she looked at him. He stirred on the seat.

"If I'd had brains enough to get married," he said, "might be I'd have had a son. Might have been one like that."

The woman looked away, out her window. She reached up to pat at her hair and the firm line of her lips softened in the tiny imperceptible beginnings of a smile. The dust drifted and the minutes passed and Sergeant Houck stirred again.

"It's the upbringing that counts," he said, and settled into silent immobility, watching the miles go by.

Fifteen minutes for breakfast at a change stop and the coach rolled on. It was near noon when they stopped in Laramie and Sergeant Houck handed the woman out and tucked the boy under one arm and led the way to the waiting room. He stationed the woman and the boy in two chairs and strode away. He was back in five minutes with sandwiches and a pitcher of milk and two cups. He strode away again and was gone longer and returned driving a light buckboard wagon drawn by a pair of deep-barrelled bays. The front part of the wagon bed was well padded with layers of empty burlap bags. He went into the waiting room and scooped up the boy and beckoned to the woman to follow. He deposited the boy on the burlap bags and helped the woman up on the driving seat.

"Straight out the road, they tell me," he said. "About fifteen miles. Then right along the creek. Can't miss it."

He stood by the wagon, staring along the length of the street and the road leading on beyond. The woman leaned from the seat and clutched at his shoulder. Her voice broke and climbed. "You're going with me?" Her fingers clung to the cloth of his service jacket. "Please! You've got to!"

Sergeant Houck put a hand over hers on his shoulder and released her fingers. "Yes, I'm going."

He walked around the wagon and stepped to the seat and took the reins and clucked to the team. The wagon moved forward and curious people along the street stopped to watch, and neither Sergeant Houck nor the woman was aware of them. The wheels rolled silently in the thick dust, and on the open road there was no sound except the small creakings of the wagon body and the muffled rhythm of the horses' hooves. A road-runner appeared from nowhere and raced ahead of them, its feet spatting little spurts of dust, and Sergeant Houck watched it running, effortlessly, always the same distance ahead.

"You're afraid," he said.

The wheels rolled silently in the thick dust and the roadrunner swung contemptuously aside in a big arc and disappeared in the low bushes.

"They haven't told him," she said, "about the boy."

Sergeant Houck's hands tightened on the reins and the horses slowed to a walk. He clucked sharply to them and slapped the reins on their backs and they quickened again into a trot, and the wheels unwound their thin tracks endlessly into the dust and the high bright sun overhead crept over and down the sky on the left. The wagon topped a slight rise and the road ahead sloped downwards for a long stretch to where the green of trees and tall bushes showed in the distance. A jack-rabbit started from the scrub growth by the roadside and leaped high in a spy-hop and levelled out, a gray-brown streak. The horses shied and broke rhythm and quieted to a walk under the firm pressure of the reins. Sergeant Houck kept them at a walk, easing the heat out of their muscles down the long slope to the trees. He let them step into the creek up to their knees and dip muzzles in the clear running water. The front wheels of the wagon were into the current and he reached behind him to find a tin dipper tucked among the burlap bags and leaned far out and down to dip up water for the woman and the boy and himself. He backed the team out of the creek and swung them into the wagon cuts leading along the bank to the right.

The creek was on their left and the sun was behind them, warm on their backs, and the shadows of the horses pushed ahead, grotesque moving patterns always ahead, and Sergeant Houck watched them and looked beside him once and saw that the woman was watching them too. The shadows were longer, stretching farther ahead, when they rounded a bend along the creek and the buildings came in sight, the two-room cabin and the several lean-to sheds and the rickety pole corral.

A man was standing by one of the sheds, and when Sergeant Houck stopped the team, he came towards them and halted about twenty feet away. He was not young, perhaps in his middle thirties, but with the young look of a man on whom the years have made no mark except that of the simple passing of time. He was tall, soft, and loose-jointed in build, and indecisive in manner and movement. His eyes wavered and would not steady as he looked at the woman and the fingers of his hands hanging limp at his sides twitched as he waited for her to speak.

She climbed down her side of the wagon and faced him. She

stood straight and the sun behind her shone on and through the escaping wisps of the coiled braid of her hair.

"Well, Fred," she said, "I'm here."

"Cora," he said. "It's been a long time, Cora. I didn't know you'd come so soon."

"Why didn't you come get me? Why didn't you, Fred?"

"I didn't rightly know what to do, Cora. It was all so mixed up. Thinking you were dead. Then hearing about you. And what happened. I had to think about things. And I couldn't get away easy. I was going to try maybe next week."

"I hoped you'd come. Right away when you heard."

His body twisted uneasily, a strange movement that stirred his whole length while his feet remained flat and motionless on the ground. "Your hair's still pretty," he said. "The way it used to be."

Something like a sob caught in her throat and she started towards him. Sergeant Houck stepped down on the other side of the wagon and strode off to the creek and kneeled to bend and wash the dust from his face. He stood, shaking the drops from his hands and drying his face with a handkerchief and watching the little eddies of the current around several stones in the creek. He heard the voices behind him and by the wagon.

"Wait, Fred. There's something you have to know—"

"That kid? What's it doing here with you?"

"It's mine, Fred."

"Yours? Where'd you get it?"

"It's my child. Mine."

Silence, and then the man's voice, bewildered, hurt. "So it's really true what they said. About that Indian."

"Yes. He bought me. By their rules I belonged to him."

Silence, and then the woman's voice again. "I wouldn't be alive and here now, any other way. I didn't have any say about it."

Silence, and then the man's voice with the faint beginning of self-pity creeping into the tone. "I didn't count on anything like this."

Sergeant Houck turned and strode back by the wagon. The woman seemed relieved at the interruption.

"This is Sergeant Houck," she said. "He brought me all the way."

The man nodded his head and raised a hand to shove back the sandy hair that kept falling forward on his forehead. "I suppose I ought to thank you, soldier. All that trouble."

"No trouble," said Sergeant Houck. "Unusual duty. But no trouble."

The man pushed at the ground in front of him with one shoe, poking the toe into the dirt and studying it. "It's silly, just standing around here. I suppose we ought to go inside. It's near suppertime. I guess you'll be taking a meal here, soldier. Before you start back to town."

"Right," said Sergeant Houck. "And I'm tired. I'll stay the night too. Start in the morning. Sleep in one of those sheds."

The man pushed at the ground more vigorously. The little dirt pile in front of his shoe seemed to interest him greatly. "All right, soldier. Sorry there're no quarters inside." He swung quickly and started for the cabin. The woman took the boy from the wagon and followed him. Sergeant Houck unharnessed the horses and led them to the creek for a drink and to the corral and let them through the gate. He walked quietly to the cabin doorway and stopped just outside. He could see the man sitting on a straight-backed chair by the table, turned away from him. The woman and the boy were out of sight to one side.

"For God's sake, Cora," the man was saying, "I don't see why you had to bring that kid with you. You could have told me about it. I didn't have to see him."

Her voice was sharp, startled. "What do you mean?"

"Why, now we've got the problem of how to get rid of him. Have to find a mission or someplace that'll take him. Why didn't you leave him where he came from?"

"No! He's mine!"

"Good God, Cora! Are you crazy? Think you can foist off a thing like that on me?"

Sergeant Houck stepped through the doorway. "It's been a time since last eating," he said. "Thought I heard something about supper." He looked around the small room and brought his gaze to bear upon the man. "I see the makings on those shelves. Come along, Mr. Sutliff. She can do without our help. A woman doesn't want men cluttering about when getting a meal. Show me your place before it gets dark."

He stood, waiting, and the man scraped at the floor with one foot and slowly rose and went with him.

They were well beyond earshot of the cabin when Sergeant Houck spoke again. "How long were you married? Before it happened?"

"Six years," said the man. "No, seven. It was seven when we lost the last place and headed this way with the train."

"Seven years," said Sergeant Houck. "And no child."

"It just didn't happen. I don't know why." The man stopped and looked sharply at Sergeant Houck. "Oh! So, that's the way you're looking at it."

"Yes," said Sergeant Houck. "Now you've got one. A son."

"Not mine," said the man. "You can talk. It's not your wife. It's bad enough thinking of taking an Indian's leavings." He wiped his lips on his sleeve and spat in disgust. "I'll be damned if I'll take his kid."

"Not his anymore. He's dead."

"Look, man. Look how it'd be. A damned little half-breed. Around all the time to make me remember what she did."

"Could be a reminder that she had some mighty hard going. And maybe came through the better for it."

"She had hard going! What about me? Thinking she was dead. Getting used to that. Maybe thinking of another woman. Then she comes back—and an Indian kid with her. What does that make me?"

"Could make you a man," said Sergeant Houck. "Think it over."

He swung away and went to the corral and leaned on the rail, watching the horses roll the sweat-itches out on the dry sod. The man went slowly down by the creek and stood on the bank, pushing at the dirt with one shoe and kicking small pebbles into the water. The sun, holding to the horizon rim, dropped suddenly out of sight and dusk swept swiftly to blur the outlines of the buildings. A lamp was lit in the cabin, and the rectangle of light through the doorway made the dusk become darkness. The woman appeared in the doorway and called and the men came their ways and converged there and went in. There was simple food on the table and the woman stood beside it. "I've already fed him," she said, and moved her head towards the door to the inner room. She sat down and they did and the three of them were intent on the plates.

Sergeant Houck ate steadily and reached to refill his plate. The man picked briefly at the food before him and stopped and the woman ate nothing at all. The man put his hands on the table edge and pushed back and rose and went to a side shelf and took a bottle and two thick cups and returned to set these by his plate. He filled the cups a third full from the bottle and shoved one along the table boards towards Sergeant Houck. He lifted the other chin-high. His voice was bitter. "Happy homecoming," he said. He waited and Sergeant Houck took the other cup and they drank. The man lifted the bottle and poured himself another cup-third.

The woman moved her chair and looked quickly at him and away.

"Please, Fred."

The man paid no attention to the words. He reached with the bottle towards the other cup.

"No," said Sergeant Houck.

The man shrugged. "You can think better on whisky. Sharpens the mind." He set the bottle down and took his cup and drained it. He coughed and put it carefully on the table in front of him and pushed at it with one forefinger. Sergeant Houck fumbled in his right-side pocket and found one of the short straight straws there and pulled it out and put one end in his mouth and chewed slowly on it. The man and the woman sat still, opposite each other at the table, and seemed to forget this quiet presence. They stared at the table, at the floor, at the cabin walls, everywhere except at each other. Yet their attention was plainly concentrated on each other across the table top. The man spoke first. His voice was restrained, carrying conscious patience.

"Look, Cora. You wouldn't want to do that to me. You can't mean what you said before."

Her voice was low, determined. "He's mine."

"Now, Cora. You don't want to push it too far. A man can take just so much. I didn't know what to do after I heard about you. But I remembered you had been a good wife. I was all ready to forgive you; And now you—"

"Forgive me!" She knocked against her chair rising to her feet. Hurt and bewilderment made her voice ragged as she repeated the words. "Forgive me?" She turned and fairly ran into the inner room. The handleless door banged shut and bounced open again inward a few inches and she leaned against it inside to close it tightly.

The man stared after her and shook his head a little and reached again for the bottle.

"Enough's enough," said Sergeant Houck.

The man became aware of him and shrugged in quick irritation. "For you, maybe," he said, and poured himself another cupthird. He thrust his head a little forward at Sergeant Houck. "Is there any reason you should be noseying in on this?"

"My orders," said Sergeant Houck, "were to deliver them safely. Both of them. Safely."

"You've done that," said the man. He lifted the cup and drained it and set it down carefully. "They're here."

"Yes," said Sergeant Houck, "they're here." He rose and stepped to the outside door and looked into the night. He waited a moment until his eyes were accustomed to the darkness and could distinguish objects faintly in the starlight. He stepped on out and went to the straw pile behind one of the sheds and took an armload and carried it back by the cabin and dropped it at the foot of a tree by one corner. He lowered his bulk to the straw and sat there, legs stretched out, shoulders against the tree, and broke off a straw stem and chewed slowly on it. After a while his jaws stopped their slow, slight movement and his head sank forward and his eyes closed.

~:~

Sergeant Houck awoke, completely, in the instant, and aware. The stars had swung perhaps an hour overhead. He was on his feet in the swift reflex, and listening. The straw rustled under his shoes and was still. He heard the faint sound of voices in the cabin, indistinct but rising as tension rose in them. He went towards the doorway and stopped just short of the rectangle of light from the still burning lamp.

"You're not going to have anything to do with me!" The woman's voice was harsh with stubborn anger. "Not until this has been settled right!"

"Aw, come on, Cora." The man's voice was fuzzy, slow-paced. "We'll talk about that in the morning."

"No!"

"All right!" Sudden fury shook the man's voice. "You want it settled now! Well, it's settled! We're getting rid of that damn kid first thing tomorrow!"

"No!"

"What gave you the idea you've got any say around here after what you did? I'm the one to say what's to be done. You don't be careful, maybe I won't take you back."

"Maybe I don't want you to take me back!"

"So damn finicky all of a sudden! After being with that Indian and maybe a lot more!"

Sergeant Houck stepped through the doorway. The man's back was to him and he put out his left hand and took hold of the man's shoulder and spun him around, and his right hand smacked against the side of the man's face and sent him staggering against the wall.

"Forgetting your manners won't help," said Sergeant Houck. He looked around and the woman had disappeared into the inner room. The man leaned against the wall rubbing his cheek, and she emerged, the boy in her arms, and ran towards the outer door.

"Cora!" the man shouted. "Cora!"

She stopped, a brief hesitation in flight. "I don't belong to you," she said, and was gone through the doorway. The man pushed out from the wall and started after her and the great hulk of Sergeant Houck blocked the way.

"You heard her," said Sergeant Houck. "She doesn't belong to anybody now. But that boy."

The man stared at him and some of the fury went out of the man's eyes and he stumbled to his chair at the table and reached for the nearly empty bottle. Sergeant Houck watched him a moment, then turned and quietly went outside. He walked towards the corral and as he passed the second shed she came out of the darker shadows and her voice, low and intense, whispered at him.

"I've got to go. I can't stay here."

Sergeant Houck nodded and went on to the corral and opened the gate and, stepping softly and chirruping a wordless little tune, approached the horses. They stirred uneasily and moved away and stopped and waited for him. He led them through the gate to the wagon and harnessed them quickly and with a minimum of sound. He finished buckling the traces and stood straight and looked towards the cabin. He walked steadily to the lighted rectangle of the doorway and stepped inside and over by the table. The man was leaning forward in his chair, elbows on the table, staring at the empty bottle.

"It's finished," said Sergeant Houck. "She's leaving now."

The man shook his head and pushed at the bottle with one forefinger. "She can't do that." He swung his head to look up at Sergeant Houck and the sudden fury began to heat his eyes. "She can't do that! She's my wife!"

"Not anymore," said Sergeant Houck. "Best forget she ever came back." He started towards the door and heard the sharp sound of the chair scraping on the floor behind him. The man's voice rose, shrilling up almost into a shriek.

"Stop!" The man rushed to the wall rack and grabbed the rifle there and swung it at his hip, bringing the muzzle to bear on Sergeant Houck. "Stop!" He was breathing deeply and he fought for control of his voice. "You're not going to take her away!"

Sergeant Houck turned slowly. He stood still, a motionless granite shape in the lamplight.

"Threatening an Army man," said Sergeant Houck. "And with an empty gun."

The man wavered and his eyes flicked down at the rifle, and in the second of indecision Sergeant Houck plunged towards him and one huge hand grasped the gun barrel and pushed it aside and the shot thudded harmlessly into the cabin wall. He wrenched the gun from the man's grasp and his other hand took the man by the shirt front and shook him forward and back and pushed him over and down into the chair.

"No more of that," said Sergeant Houck. "Best sit quiet." His eyes swept the room and found the box of cartridges on a shelf and he took this with the rifle and went to the door. "Look around in the morning and you'll find these." He went outside and tossed the gun up on the roof of one of the sheds and dropped the little box by the straw pile and kicked straw over it. He went to the wagon and stood by it and the woman came out of the darkness of the trees by the creek, carrying the boy.

༒

The wagon wheels rolled silently and the small creakings of the wagon body and the thudding rhythm of the horses' hooves were distinct, isolated sounds in the night. The creek was on their right and they followed the tracing of the road back the way they had come. The woman moved on the seat, shifting the boy's weight from one arm to the other, and Sergeant Houck took him by the overalls and lifted him and reached behind to lay him on the burlap bags.

"A good boy," he said. "Has the Indian way of taking things without yapping. A good way."

The thin new tracks in the dust unwound endlessly under the wheels and the late waning moon climbed out of the horizon and its light shone in pale, barely noticeable patches through the scattered bushes and trees along the creek.

"I have relatives in Missouri," said the woman. "I could go there."

Sergeant Houck fumbled in his side pocket and found a straw and put this in his mouth and chewed slowly on it "Is that what you want?"

"No."

They came to the main road crossing and swung left and the dust thickened under the horses' hooves. The lean dark shape of a coyote slipped from the brush on one side and bounded along the road and disappeared on the other side.

"I'm forty-seven," said Sergeant Houck. "Nearly thirty of that in the Army. Makes a man rough."

The woman looked straight ahead at the far dwindling ribbon of the road and a small smile curled the corners of her mouth.

"Four months," said Sergeant Houck, "and this last hitch is done. I'm thinking of homesteading on out in the Territory." He chewed on the straw and took it between a thumb and forefinger and flipped it away. "You could get a room at the settlement."

"I could," said the woman. The horses slowed to a walk, breathing deeply, and he let them hold the steady, plodding pace. Far off a coyote howled and others caught the signal and the sounds echoed back and forth in the distance and died away into the night silence.

"Four months," said Sergeant Houck. "That's not so long."

"No," said the woman. "Not too long."

A breeze stirred across the brush and took the dust from the slow hooves in small whorls and the wheels rolled slowly and she put out a hand and touched his shoulder. The fingers moved down along his upper arm and curved over the big muscles there and the warmth of them sank through the cloth of his worn service jacket. She dropped the hand again in her lap and looked ahead along the ribbon of the road. He clucked to the horses and urged them again into a trot, and the small creakings of the wagon body and the dulled rhythm of the hooves were gentle sounds in the night.

The wheels rolled and the late moon climbed, and its pale light shone slantwise down on the moving wagon, on the sleeping boy, and on the woman looking straight ahead and the great granite slab of Sergeant Houck.

Kittura Remsberg

Kittura Remsberg was my grandmother. My mother's mother. I knew her only the few weeks I spent at the ranch near Kalispell one summer, and then only as little more than a presence, dark eyes and still dark hair above the prominent cheekbones of a permanent invalid held to her bed within the walls of the room that compassed all that remained of her life. It was a big room, big and quiet and cool even when the summer sun burned the wide reaches of the range outside. I was in it only the few times she asked for me. I never went in voluntarily because I was afraid of her. She was not a storybook grandmother. She was an impatient, sharp-tongued personality with no softness for me in her. Yet I remember that room with a clarity and a feeling that spring unfailing across the years. I remember it because she was there and she filled it with a bigness and a quietness and a strange cool strength of spirit. There was peace in that room.

I would not have spent those weeks at the ranch if my parents had not been hard-pressed and unable to hire a nurse when my sister had rheumatic fever. They felt I should be sent away for a while and there was no place else to send me. They worried for days before they did send me because my mother disapproved of

Ben Remsberg, her father, my grandfather. She had married early to get away and into town and not be dependent on him. She said that he drank too much and that he had a violent temper. She said that no decent person who could get away would live long in the same house with him. From her point of view perhaps she was right. I saw him drunk more than once during those few weeks and heard him shout in frequent fury at the fat old Mexican woman who did the housework and at the one old cowhand who had stayed with him. But he was kind to me and let me tag him about asking endless questions. And he told me about the woman, his wife, my grandmother, lying quietly in the big cool room.

There was nothing peculiar about his telling me, though my mother always said he was difficult to talk to. He told me because I asked him. I asked him because I noticed he was different when he went into that room. He was loud and angry much of the time outside of it. But when he passed through that doorway he was different. He usually closed the door after him, and then for a while after he came out he would be soft-spoken and absent-minded as if he were out of focus with things immediately around him. Once he left the door partly open and I peered in. He was sitting on a chair by the bed with one of his broad blunt hands resting on the counterpane beside her and she was sitting in the bed with her back to a pillow and one of her thin hands was on his hand and they were just sitting there together. When he came out I asked him about her and he told me. He told me about her and about the mirror, and I saw it once in the loft of the storage barn, the heavy gilt paint of the ornate frame chipping off and only a few pieces of jagged glass left in one corner.

The whole story has come clear in my mind through the years. Some of the details and spoken words may not be true to absolute exact fact. But the whole of it means truth to me. Kittura Remsberg was my grandmother and I want to tell you about her.

～∶～

Kittura Perkins was her maiden name. She was the third daughter of a prosperous landowner in Pennsylvania about thirty miles out of Philadelphia. He was a man of real substance in his part of the State. They lived in the main farmhouse on the property where he could hold sharp watch on his crops and see that the hired men earned their keep. He also owned a share in a shipping business in the city and he had filled the farmhouse with fine furniture brought from Europe at bargain intervals by his company's ships. His wife, Kittura's mother, had died when she was small, and the two older sisters had done their futile best to raise her as a proper young lady.

Kitt Perkins everyone called her during those years just after the Civil War, and she knew everyone in the neighborhood and everyone knew her as a strong-willed girl whose vital coloring and manner contrasted sharply with the pallid gentility of her sisters and whose habits of going her own way and speaking her own mind annoyed her careful father. The young men knew her and wanted to know her better. She herself was constantly disappointed in them. She knew what she wanted and one day she saw it.

What she saw was a deep-bodied young man lifting an anvil out of a wagon and setting it on the ground and kneeling to hammer horseshoes into shape on it with slow deliberate strokes. He was the son of a Belgian immigrant who had come into the neighborhood some years before and set up a blacksmith shop. She had seen him often helping his father, but now she really saw him for the first time. She liked the shape of him, solid and thick through.

She liked the way he looked at her, measuring her without offense as a healthy human animal whose vitality might match his own. She did not like the way he kept silent, withdrawing as if he realized a gap between them.

She went straight to him. "Why won't you speak to me?"

He laid the hammer on the anvil and looked up at her. "That wouldn't do anybody any good. I'm not your kind."

"That's ridiculous."

"Yes? Your father wouldn't like it."

"Ben Remsberg," she said, "I am not my father."

~∴~

That was the beginning. They were together each evening after that for nearly two weeks. They walked the fields long miles that seemed short, often talking eagerly and as often being silent and content to be. Then one evening she stopped and looked straight at him. "I want you to call on me tomorrow night. At home."

He came, and he was awkward in his dress-up clothes. He was uncomfortable talking to her in the fine parlor. He was more uncomfortable when her sisters stepped in to be introduced and made a point of departing quickly upstairs. He stood stiffly at attention when her father entered and greeted him coldly, and in the midst of a tight silence he turned and walked steadily out and down the flat stone path towards the road.

She sat silent, hurt anger rising, and then there was no anger and she ran after him. She called from the front stoop and he went steadily on and she caught him by the picket gate and swung him around. "Ben, don't be a fool."

He took her by the arms and shook her fiercely and her head rose defiantly and he pulled her to him. She came reaching for him, and as she felt the hard-crushing strength of his body, she knew that she was right.

She stepped back, chewing on her lower lip. "Ben, be honest with me. Are you afraid of my father?"

"No, but he doesn't want me in his house so I'll never set foot in it again."

"Then I won't either."

He stared at her, startled. "Where will you go?"

"Wherever you go."

"But—but I oughtn't to marry you."

"Why not?"

"No money, that's why. I haven't got anything."

"Ben," she said, "you'll have me."

~:~

They were married that night. They sent word to her father and went home to the little house behind the blacksmith shop and his father blessed them in his flowing French and moved into the room over the shop and they were alone in the little house together. In the morning he was tall with arrogance of possession and she was certain that she was right. She was so certain of many things.

"Ben, we'll have to set foot in father's house again, after all. To get my clothes. And of course, my mirror."

They drove a wagon to the big farmhouse and her sisters watched in disapproving silence while they carried out the contents of her old mahogany wardrobe. He was surprised when he saw the mirror. It was full-length, tall enough for the tallest man, cased in a heavy frame, hand-carved and gilt-painted. He had to rest often lugging it down the stairs and to the wagon. And all the while she talked, telling him about it. "I've had it ever since I was a little girl. Father had it brought from England, some old place there, and I made such a fuss he said I could have it. I like to sit with it. Fixing myself and thinking. That's how I first knew you were the man I'd marry. Oh, not you, of course, then. Someone like you."

And when he carried it into their little house, the ceiling of their bedroom was too low for it to stand upright and he had to rig a way to fasten it sideways on the wall where it looked strange and grotesque until she covered the heavy carvings of the top and bottom, now the sides, with cloth like curtains, and it was a part of the room, giving depth like a seeing into and beyond the confining walls.

~:~

They lived quietly to themselves and for the first months being together was enough. But the blacksmith shop was small. Most of its meagre business came from the poorer farmers who lived nearby. They would barely have scraped along except for the small income she had from her mother's estate. Then one morning he and his father were repairing the cracked axle of a loaded grain cart and suddenly the cart crumpled and overturned, sending him sprawling and pinning his father under the weight of the piled bags. Three days his father lay in the bedroom watching the mirror catch the sun through the one window and on the third day died, apologetic to his last breath over the trouble he had caused. And money was a bit easier for them after the funeral expenses because all that came into the shop was theirs.

Easier. Not easy enough. Ben Remsberg was no businessman, not in the cautious penny-watching way of the people with whom he had to deal. He used better materials and did better work

136

than most of his customers paid for. He could not refuse a call on his time even from a man already behind in paying for past work. At the end of the month he would be short on the rent for the shop and the house and it would be her money that matched the amount. For the next days he would be irritable and too harsh demanding payment and his mouth would be tight in a straight line.

Then one evening she looked at him over the supper dishes and chewed on her lower lip. "Ben, you don't want to be a blacksmith all your life, do you?"

He stared down at his empty plate, searching his own mind for her. "No. And not here. When I was a kid, I used to think some of striking out somewhere for myself."

"Why didn't you?"

"Oh, I don't know. First there was papa. Now there's you."

She looked at him, serious and perhaps a bit frightened. "Ben, be honest with me. What do you want to do with your life?"

"I guess I want to be some place where it's new. Where a man can start with nothing and show what he is. I've thought some of going West."

She chewed on her lip a long moment. She remembered many things out of the passing days, little things like his sullen naming of a price for a poor farmer when his impulse was to give freely of himself in open fellowship. She remembered the wideness of him, the stretching bigness that was not of his body alone and that seemed to be shrinking at each month's end. She remembered and spoke quickly to have it said.

"You ought to do it, Ben. Go West or wherever you want."

He stared at her, startled. "You mean just do it? Just like that?"

"Yes. That's the way to do things. Or else you might never do them."

"But—but you don't mean go and leave you?"

"I mean go find where you want to be and come back and get me."

"But—but a man can't—"

"Ben, don't ever let me be in your way."

~:~

He left her in the morning, swinging down the road to Philadelphia and a start on the first train west with an extra shirt and several pairs of socks in a neat bundle under his arm. She watched him go and turned back into the house and closed the door, and with it closed a period in her life and began another, the years of being alone.

Four years. Four years and some months. She sold the equipment in the shop and rented the building to an elderly farmer for a small grocery store. With that and her own income she was independent. She waited and sat hours in front of the mirror and steadied her mind against the waiting with thoughts of the fine big home they would build, somewhere, sometime. And she saved what she could of the money available and bought things they would need for that home. Bedclothes and linens and dishes, and on rare occasions pieces of silver. She took wooden boxes from the store and packed the things in these, snugly packed and repacked for the journey to wherever they would be together.

With Ben gone, she began to see her family again. Once a month her sisters came to call in the family carriage. They came with a sense of duty and did not disguise the fact that they were sorry for her, and they never stayed long because she never let them see that she might be sorry for herself. Once a week her father came. He would knock on the door, and when she opened it he would take off his hat and say: "Well, Kittura, are you ready to come home now?" And when she would shake her head, he would turn and walk away in stubborn wonderment.

A few weeks after Ben left, a card came from Cincinnati. He was working his way on a river boat and moving West. Later there was another from St. Louis. He was moving on by rail tending a carload of herd bulls and thought there might be a ranch job at the end of the line. That was all. And the months stretched into years, and the note came, the hurried scrawl: "Forget about me. I'm not your kind."

She sat by the mirror and read the note again and again. She took a piece of paper and a pencil and wrote on the paper and chewed on her lower lip and wrote again. She tore the paper across and dropped it on the floor and took another piece and wrote a single line on it. "Ben," she wrote, "don't be a fool." She tucked this piece in an envelope and saw the Fort Laramie postmark on his note and addressed her envelope to him care of General Delivery there and walked to the post office and mailed it. The months passed and she sat by the mirror and saw the straightness growing in her lips, and she cut expenses more to buy more things for the boxes beginning to fill the front room of the little house. And after four years and some months he was there, suddenly and completely and travel-worn in the doorway with her paper in his hand.

"Kitt, I came damn near being a fool. This caught up with me and I pulled in sharp. Got me a stake and found a place."

"A place, Ben? Is it what you want?"

"Yes. A nice piece of range off near the mountains where nobody's spoiled it. I've got a few mavericks on it already."

"Mavericks, Ben?"

"Sure. Calves. Orphans. No one to claim them. I scoured them out of the bush and slapped my brand on them. Our brand. A straight big K."

He was sunburned and rugged with the hard fitness of tough cordwood. He stood in the doorway, a man who owned the earth in company with all men who were men. She felt the wideness spreading out from him. She dropped into a chair and her shoulders shook as the sobs fought in her throat. He leaped to kneel beside her and put out his arms and she gripped him with fingers that dug into his welcome hardness.

"Ben," she kept saying, "Ben. I was right after all, wasn't I, Ben?"

She let him sleep late in the morning while she cooked a good breakfast and she waited until he had eaten. Then she could wait no longer and hurried to show him her boxes. He followed from one to the next and on to them all, and amazement grew in him till it burst out in a shout that shook the house.

"Good God, Kitt! All that stuff! It's wonderful! But do you realize where you're going? Way out to the end of nowhere. It's four hundred miles from the nearest railhead. All I've got anyway is a two-room shack. We're starting small, Kitt."

"Suppose we are. We won't always be small. We'll be building a decent place."

"Sure. That'll come. But we've got no use for stuff like this now. What we need is good breeding cows and a couple of the right kind of range bulls."

"I just don't care, Ben. These things are going with us. We'll keep them till we can use them. I'll get mother's money from the bank and we'll send them by train and buy wagons for the rest of the way."

"Why, I bet you'd even try to take that mirror."

"Of course. Especially my mirror."

~:~

They waited five weeks for the shipment at the railhead out of Corinne in Utah Territory. She had time after the excitement of the long train trip to become accustomed to the change in all that had been familiar. She learned to endure the dust and the heat that swirled by day through the one street of the crowded town and the night-time noise that penetrated the room over a saloon that was the only one they could find. She was even proud of Ben in his worn Western clothes with a gun at his side and meeting and mingling with strange kinds of men in easy equality. But it was then that the fear began to creep into her, not a physical fear but a far-back shrinking from the newness and rawness and sprawling bigness of the land. She clung in her mind to the thought of her boxes coming and with them the wide flat crate that held the mirror, the tangible evidences of the life she had known that she would be taking with her. She was reassured when the things came and were stowed with their supplies in two heavy wagons and they headed north, she and Ben and her boxes and the two teams pulling the wagons and the lank silent prospector who was driving one to pay his way northward to the mining country. They moved along rapidly the first days and crossed into Idaho and pushed steadily north until the ground began to drop into the valley of the Snake River and they reached the south bank and followed upstream to cross at Fort Hall.

They had to wait two more weeks there because reports of Indian raids were drifting down country and military orders were that no wagons could travel except in companies of ten or more. When they started again, part of a long various procession of vehicles, their driver disappeared the first night out, disappeared into the darkness, and why and what happened to him they never knew, and she had to drive their second wagon after that, wincing at the grind of the hard leather until the callouses formed on her hands.

The season was far advanced by now. Grass for the horses was sparse and burned and water was often more than a full day's drive ahead. Day merged into day as the motley procession climbed the long rolling rise out of the valley and struck across the high plateau towards the mountains and the Montana line and the safety of Bannack City. Twice the company's lone point rider reported Indian signs and once they saw smoke signals rising far off in the horizon haze. The men drove for all possible distance each daylight hour and grew ever more grim in the circle of wagons at night. The nameless fear of the new land crept into her again, and she might have begged Ben to turn back if turning back would not have been worse than going forward. Their horses straining long days into the tugs of the heavy wagons, wasted down to a weakening thinness and slowed in pace until she and Ben dropped back place by place in the procession and were among the last stragglers to reach camp at night. And then, in the forenoon of one day so relentlessly like the others, the fear took her.

They had reached a rocky dry gulch where they had expected to find at least a trickle of water still running. There were only dust and caked mud and the bare stones baking in the sun. The other wagons had crossed the dry ford and were pushing on. She had seen Ben, showing her the way for their own wagons as he always did, swing his team to hit the crossing at an angle and avoid the biggest stones. She followed and tried to do the same, and as the horses settled to the pull up the other side a rear wheel struck a rock and the wagon stopped. She urged the team sideways and forward and heard the wheel grind on the rock and drop back immovable. She saw the other wagons moving on, the distance growing, and the fear rushed through her. Frantically she slapped at the horses with the reins and they lunged forward and one of them floundered in the loose gravel of the slope and went down.

She saw the horse fight upward and stand with one leg hanging useless and her scream brought men upright and pulling in their teams all along the line ahead.

She sat on the seat silent and unable to move. She saw Ben standing beside the wagon and staring at her and at the horse and then walking to meet the other men coming and stand with them in hurried talk. She saw them scatter towards their own wagons and Ben coming towards her. He looked up and managed a small tight smile for her. "This does it, Kitt. We tried anyway. Wait for me at the other wagon."

At the sound of his voice she could move and she climbed down and went forward and pulled herself up to the other driving seat. She did not dare look around until after the shot, and when she did turn he was leading the other horse unharnessed and tying it by the bridle to the tailboard behind her. She looked back at the wagon in the gulch piled with her boxes beneath the dusty canvas.

She spoke softly in simple wonder. "I don't understand, Ben. What are we going to do? Will we tow it?"

"Good God, Kitt! We're going to leave it. Damn near everything else too."

The words hit her mind, but she did not grasp them until he began to pull boxes out of the wagon bed behind her and heave them to one side. Then the fear raced through her again and she jumped to the ground and ran headlong at him and beat at him with her hands. "You can't, Ben! You can't!"

He held her from him, shaking her by the arms. "Listen, Kitt. We're miles from anywhere. No water. Horses about played out. Indians maybe near. We have to travel light and might not make it even then."

"No! You can't!" She broke from him and blocked him from the wagon. "I won't have anything left! Not anything!" Her voice rose wailing and he snapped at her in contempt. "If they can, we can." She looked and saw the other men stripping down their wagons and some of the women helping, and she was suddenly ashamed and stepped aside. She stood quietly while he stripped the wagon to the sparse necessities—food and a few tools and the two rifles and several blankets—and she drove away the fear that was not a physical fear, and the conviction came. He was throwing away her defenses against the brutal indifference of this raw land, and if she let this happen she would be alone in a strange nakedness and she would lose contact with a way of life she could never recapture.

When he finished, she spoke quietly. "All right, Ben. I won't make any more fuss. But you've forgotten my mirror." When he stared at her, she spoke again quietly, "I'll leave everything else, but I won't leave that. If we can't take it, I'll stay here too." When he still stared at her, she spoke again just as quietly, "Ben, I mean it."

~:~

When they moved on, more rapidly now and the last in the long line driving for distance, he sat beside her grim and refusing to look at her as he had been getting the wide flat crate from the abandoned wagon and struggling with it end over end up the slope. She sat huddled on the seat beside him in her own taut silence, and the hours crawled by and she watched the barren burned miles passing under the horses' hooves, and for the first time when they were together they were not together and they lay apart in separate blankets that night, not sleeping and perhaps not hearing the lonely night sounds.

It was the same in the morning. She watched the dust rising under the hooves and moving backwards under the wagon, and with each passing hour the effort to speak became more difficult. Then her head began to rise and a faint suggestion of freshness touched the air, and far ahead almost beyond vision the haze began to shift and take shapes and was no longer haze, but the remote challenging solidity of the mountains. And when speaking no longer seemed possible she spoke: "I was wrong, Ben. I have you."

He swung his head to look at her and some of the grimness left his face. Speaking was easier now and her voice gained strength.

"I was wrong too about bringing all those things. I should have saved the money and we'd have some now for you to buy your cattle."

He sat up straighter on the seat and clucked to the horses. "Just as well, Kitt. Now we're starting right."

She nodded and watched the mountains emerging in sharper outline. "I guess, Ben, I just couldn't accept all this new way of doing things. This—this land. It's so big, and it doesn't seem to know that we're even here. But you don't need to worry about me anymore."

"I'm not worrying," he said. "Not about you." And they were together on the seat, gaunt and tired and dusty in a creaking wagon at the tag end of a motley worn procession, but together. He stirred on the seat and licked his dry lips and grinned a little. "That mirror. I guess we've got to take it through somehow if I have to carry the damned thing."

They took it through. Flat in the wagon bed, the wide crate was a seat for two families whose own wagons had broken past repair during the last days before they rolled into Bannack City. It was there, firm ballast in the bottom, when they struck on north through the mountains to Butte and on past Deer Lodge and Gold Creek to Fort Missoula. It was there, almost the only thing left to unload, when they reached the Flathead Lake country and stopped at last by the shack that was their home for the next years.

Nothing, no trick of curtains, could make that mirror be anything but grotesque in that shack. It was out of place, out of keeping, an unbelievable burst of elegance out of another world. Yet there was a rightness in its very wrongness. It was a symbol and a signpost. A reminder and a beckoning. And certainly, it was a mark of distinction. It made them quickly known through the Territory, the "looking-glass people," and the word ran and far neighbors came miles to see it. Hung sideways again, it nearly filled one end of the main room of the shack, eye-holding and impressive, and it hung there during the years they put themselves and everything possible into the ranch, reaching out, buying land and cattle, taking long chances on slim credit and always somehow pulling through, the two of them together, seen and known by everyone and always together. And then things were easy for them. He had what he wanted, miles of good range and hundreds of cattle on it, and she could have what she wanted, a house to match the mirror.

Building that house must have been an event in that growing Territory. While she was still planning it, word came that her father had died and she could draw on a third of his estate and they tossed discretion aside and built the house big, rambling and roomy with wide walls and deep-set windows and high-ceilinged with huge beams freighted down from the mountain forests. And she bought and bought things for it, sending as far as Denver and even all the way to New York for them, feeling that at last in a sense she had again and was unpacking her wooden boxes. Together they had defeated the land that had almost defeated her, and her house was her victory banner, what she had once had and known remade for her. She filled it with fine things as her father had his house, and when she was finished the mirror stood upright in their bedroom and merged into the over-all magnificence.

Her one child was born in that bedroom. One. There were no others. Perhaps that bothered her as sometimes it bothered Ben, but it did not mar the running rightness of their being together. They kept open house for all the surrounding country and lived smack up to the edge of their income and beyond and never worried because they had put that behind them years and miles before on the hard board seat of a dust-covered wagon. With heads high and eyes forward they lived straight into the bitter winter of '86.

~:~

Summer came early that year, dry and warm. As it progressed, hot winds swept through the valleys and the grass was stunted and shrivelled back on its roots. Droughts far down in the southwest sent extra numbers of cattle north and Ben jumped at the low prices and rented more range and bought till this too was crowded. As fall came he held his herds late, hoping for a rise in the market, and then it was too late. Winter dropped out of the mountains six weeks earlier than usual and gripped the land with a blizzard that blocked all movement. Deadly cold settled and stayed, and as the weeks passed blizzard after blizzard buried even the level stretches under four or five feet of dry packing snow. When the first thaw broke in mid-March, the overflowing streams were choked with the emaciated bodies of dead cattle. When the snow had gone down enough for an attempt at a spring round-up, there were only a few pitiful survivors where thousands had grazed.

Days passed and their men were paid off somehow and drifted away, and Ben Remsberg sat and looked out over the ruined land and Kitt Remsberg wandered through her big house and sat by the mirror chewing on her lower lip.

She went to him and sat beside him. "How bad is it, Ben?"

"We're wiped out. Not enough left to pay taxes. And we still owe on cattle lying dead out there. We'll be lucky to hold on to your house." He tried a grin for her and it was worn and thin like the feeling coming from him. "I guess I can always be a blacksmith again."

"Ben, what would it take to lick winters like that?"

"Only one way, Kitt. Wind shelters. Plenty of hay for the rough times when the grass is covered. That would take money. For lumber and equipment and barn space. We haven't got it."

"We've got a lot of things in this house that cost a lot of money."

He stared at her, startled. "You—you'd—you mean—"

"I mean we can strip down this house the way you did a wagon once. We can tear down part of it, too, and use the lumber. We'll sell everything in it and start small again."

He stared at her and he grinned again, and she felt the wideness beginning to spread again beside her. "Everything, Kitt?"

"Well, no. Of course not. Not my mirror."

⁓⦂⦁⦂⁓

Together they did it, went back to the beginning and began again. They sold everything for what they could get, everything except the mirror and beds for themselves and the little girl, and they paid most of their debts and he made what other furniture they needed out of old boards, rough and crude but adequate. They ripped down more than half of the house and built their first hay barn and the first of their wind shelters. They sold part of their range and bought the small first of their new herds and a used mower and dump-rake. They worked together and progress was slow now, but they moved ahead, and the mirror stood lonely against the wall of their bedroom, but not grotesque in the emptiness of the bare room because it was still the beginning that could always be made again. And then, when they were solidly on their feet again, came the one blow that could break them.

She was riding out to find Ben across the vast stretch of level ground they kept for hay. Life sang in her and she urged the horse into full gallop and it stumbled in a small gully hidden in the tall grass and went to its knees and she pitched forward over its head and rolled with the momentum to crumple unconscious against a rock. Hours later he found the riderless horse by the home corral gate. Still later he found her, struggling towards him, clutching at the tough grasses to drag herself along in limp agony. There was little any doctor could do except ease her pain. She had fractured the base of her spine and she endured the hard cast for months, and when the pain left and the bone knit, the paralysis came, freezing the lower half of her body in a wasting immobility.

She lay in their big bedroom and drove out the despair and hopelessness. She learned to order her household through the two Mexican women Ben hired to do for her. She held to their ranch through the hours Ben spent with her telling her about it. The months moved inevitably, and she lay in the bedroom and watched the slow changes creep into Ben and herself and their house. She saw them and she refused to see them. She shut them away in her mind and willed herself to believe that nothing of importance was changed. She lay there at night with Ben beside her and waited until he breathed with the long slow regularity of sleep and she could force herself to believe that everything was as it had been because they were there together. But the morning was always bad, the time when he left her, when she watched him disappear through the doorway. And then she discovered what the mirror could do.

Lying there, looking over the foot of the bed, she had been able to see the top of it against the far wall, the carved gilt top of the frame and a small part of the glass. Now she found that when she was raised up to sit against the pillows, she could see almost all of it and it reflected for her the view through the wide window of the side wall. It was thus itself a window, a vista for her vision into the outside world showing part of the broad porch across the front of the house and the curving lane, and beyond that a corner of the barn and the corral beside it, and farther beyond that the stretching reaches of grassland. It carried her out through the confining walls into the world Ben entered when he left the room. She could be out there with him in her thoughts. And looking out through the mirror she could watch when he moved unknowing into the frame of her vision. She could try to determine, from his appearance or actions or something carried, what he was doing, what was happening about the place. Then she could surprise him with what she knew when he came into this other world, their room, to be with her. This was her secret, her solace, her defense. The mirror was her shield until it betrayed her.

She sat in the bed and watched Ben standing on the porch and the other figure appear from somewhere on some errand, the younger of the Mexican women, and stop by him, close and conscious of the closeness. She saw but could not hear them talking and the woman turned away and tossed her head in a quick provocative sidewise glance and he took her by the shoulders and swung her around and pulled her to him. She saw the two figures molded as one in the single intensity and they separated slightly and moved away together out of the mirror, out of the rigid limits of her vision.

⌒:⌒

150

Kittura Remsberg lay limp against the pillows of the bed and stared across the room at the mirror. Faithfully it held open its vista into the world outside, but she did not see that. She saw there the slow changes that had been creeping into them, into Ben and herself, and that she had refused to see. She saw the lines deepening about his mouth and his temper thinning to snap ever more easily. She saw his pity for her changing, unaware, to pity for himself and the bitterness taking him. She saw herself becoming irritable, sharp-tongued, wanting and demanding to know what he did every moment he was out of the room. She saw herself slipping into resentment of him, of his untouched vitality, his ability to stand erect and move about and go through the doorway away from her. She saw these things happening and it had taken the mirror-caught sight of two figures fusing into one in a simple elemental hunger to tell her why. She lay against the pillows and her hands beat at the cover over the thin immobility of her hips and she chewed on her lower lip till it was raw with the blood showing. Yet she was still and her voice was quiet when at last he was there by the bed looking down at her.

"I want to tell you something, Ben. My mirror. You've never noticed, but from here it lets me see right out that window. Almost the same as if I could be out there."

"That's fine, Kitt. But I've been thinking maybe I could rig some kind of a special wheelchair. Then you could—"

"No, Ben. I'll never leave this room." And while he stared at her she spoke quickly to have it said. "I saw you. In the mirror. With that woman."

Deeper color climbed behind the burned brown of his face, but his voice was as steady as hers. "I'm sorry, Kitt."

"That I saw you? That had to be." He started to speak and she stopped him with a shake of her head. "Ben, give me your gun."

He looked down at her for a long moment.

"Ben, my life is my own. Give me your gun."

He looked down at her, and he knew the quality of her and he was man enough for her to lift the gun from the holster by his side and lean to place it in her hands.

She lay against the pillows with the gun in her lap. "Ben, be honest with me. Would it be better for you if I were out of the way?"

Time moved past them and small drops of sweat stood out on his forehead as he pushed deep into his own mind.

"No, Kitt. I need you. I need to know that you are. Without that there'd be no meaning in my life."

A small sigh came from her and she looked at him and felt the wideness reaching out, wavering and twisted perhaps from the beating of the years, but a wideness for her to feel.

"All right, Ben," she said. "This is our room and all I can have. I don't want ever to see anything that you do outside of this room. I don't even want to know what you do, except about our ranch and what you want to tell me."

She did not falter as she raised the big gun and it bucked in her hand. The roar of the shot echoed from the walls and the mirror shattered in its ornate carved frame and when the last piece fell tinkling to the floor there was an abiding quietness in the room.

⌒∶∽

Kittura Remsberg was my grandmother. She is buried under a stone of mountain granite on the slight rise of ground behind the corral of the ranch that belongs to someone else now. There is another stone beside hers. I believe that Ben Remsberg, her

152

husband, my grandfather, told her the truth when he looked down at her as she lay in the bed with the big gun in her lap. When I saw him at the simple funeral, he still seemed broad and strong, rugged as an oak that sheds the years like water. Yet within a year after he raised the stone on her grave, he lay down in their bed to sleep and slipped quietly away without waking in the now empty peace of that room.

Major Burl

"You call this a town?" says the man from Homer's Crossing. "Why, a thirsty jackass that knew its way around wouldn't stop off here to sniff a rain-barrel." He stomps out so heavy the whole shack shakes.

The five men left there look at the floor. "Hell 'n' Marier," says Pumper Pete. "One of us ought of called him on that."

Big Joe squirms in his chair and takes to pushing his bottle with a finger on the table in front of him.

"Yep," says Jim Farrango. "Burl's Gulch is more a town already than the Crossing'll ever be."

"Certain is," says Pumper Pete. "An' that galoot talks thataway an' nary one of us pips a squeak. What's wrong with us?"

"I'll tell you what's wrong," says Major Burl, puffing slow behind his bar. "I can speak free about the Gulch because it's more my place than anyone else's. Bears my name. Tagged after my emporium here. I'll stretch up and be counted in it any time the trumpet blows. But it ain't a town."

"Easy, Major," says Pumper Pete. "Maybe you have got more sense than the rest of us boggled together. Leastways you can stitch words in a string so they sound mighty important. But you're stumblin' now. The Gulch has everything a town needs. There's your place here an' there's Murray's store. There's a stage stoppin' in an' gold goin' out. There's eleven claims staked close and maybe a dozen more up the creek. Must be more'n forty head of us when the tally's full."

"And a couple women," says Jim Farrango.

"Certain are," says Pumper Pete. "My old woman an' Big Joe's squaw."

"We've got all that," says the Major. "We're even marked as a post stop. Burl's Gulch is on the map. But it ain't a town."

"So," says Storekeeper Murray. "So, what is a town, Major?"

"A town," says the Major, "is more than a batch of buildings. It's more than a place where people live. It's a place where they live together. It's a place where things happen. Things that count."

"Plenty things happen here," says Pumper Pete. "You know that, Major. Most of 'em happen here in this shack."

"Those things don't count," says the Major. "They ain't permanent and abiding. A town is a place where things happen that make folks know they're partners in this ornery business of living and all wear the same brand of the human race."

"Good stitchin'," says Pumper Pete. "But too fancy for my mind. Try it simple. Name off a thing or two."

The Major tugs at his chins. "What we need," he says, "is something to pull us together. Might be a parade could do it."

He heaves to his feet behind his bar. "Dogdamn it, men," he says, "we'll do it! A week come Wednesday will be the Fourth! We'll unfurl Old Glory over Burl's Gulch with a parade they'll hear all the way to the Crossing!"

Inside the week the plans are pushing a finish. The Major gives the orders and the Committee of Three sees that the roster is complete. Pumper Pete does the talking. Jim Farrango and Big

156

Joe supply the backing. They line up every man in the Gulch and along the creek to the main bend. They are plenty persuasive, Pumper Pete talking fast with Jim on one side smiling quiet and rubbing the handle of the gun in his belt and Big Joe on the other side scowling straight ahead and cracking his big knuckles like his hands are itching to be doing something mean.

But once the idea gets around and across, not much persuading is needed. Seems as if the Gulchers have just been aching for the feel of being a town. The only catch that develops is when Woolhead Sam, handyman at Murray's store, offers his own ante. He wants to ride his mule in the procession and Jim Farrango baulks.

"For myself," says Jim, "I wouldn't pay no mind. But my pappy home in Tennessee would rise out of his grave was I to ride in the same parade with a black man."

Sam looks sorrowful at Jim. He always likes to be near Jim ever since Jim puts a bullet through the whip arm of a teamster who is ragging him for being slow with a store order. Sam is little and bent and older than anyone knows. But he is a big man inside.

"Don't go afrettin', Jim," he says. "I'll just stand by an' watch. Somebody's got to do the yellin'."

Jim clamps teeth on his cigar and glares at the Major. "Damn it," he says, "Sam's a Gulcher too. Guess I can talk back to a spirit even if it's my pappy. Sam's in."

"He's in," says the Major. "He's riding that mule and carrying the colors. He's tipped us a notion too. Who ever heard of a parade that nobody watched? Pete, there's the spot for the womenfolk. We'll use my front steps for the reviewing stand. You get the ladies primed to cheer when we step right smart."

They step right smart all right when the time arrives. They form up the creek in the cedar woods. Smack on noon by Storekeeper Murray's stemwinder they come along the wagon tracks.

The Major is in the lead, sitting his sorrel in his best show at military posting, his belly bumping the saddle horn but his shoulders square and his face stem and dignified.

Woolhead Sam is next, bareback on his mule with the butt end of the flat stick poked in his left boot-top, and the cloth folds waving over his head. Behind him is the Committee of Three, straight in their saddles and trying to make their horses step dainty and high.

Then comes Storekeeper Murray perched on the seat of his flatbed wagon, clucking to his team and holding with one, hand to the silk topper he has dug somewhere out of his stock. He has trimmed the wagon in red and white cloth and has a blue-covered pedestal in the middle of it on which is fastened the stuffed eagle that usually sits on the top shelf behind his main counter.

The rest of the Gulchers follow, three abreast, scrubbed and brushed and greased till they almost shine in the sun. They are keeping fair time to the rhythm young Mel Osborn is beating out on a whisky keg he has hung around his neck and bumping against his stomach as he walks.

The Major leads them to the lower ford and doubles them back to the reviewing stand. He eases off his horse and hoists himself to the top step beside the women. The men gather by the bottom step and he soars into fancy oratory. He starts with the thirteen colonies and the Declaration of Independence. He sweeps from the rock-ribbed coasts of Maine to the sun-swept slopes of California. He wraps himself and the Gulchers in the flag and makes even the stuffed eagle scream. When his breath is gone, he wipes his brow and drops to an ordinary pitch. "Well, boys," he says, "I've done my derndest. You take over."

Then all of them, forty-two by Pumper Pete's tally, unloose the huzzas. Guns pop out of pockets and belts and boot tops and begin to pepper the tree branches. For a pair of minutes Burl's

Gulch is one big echoing noise. The silence after is deep and impressive.

Everyone is still savoring it when the delegation arrives. The man from Horner's Crossing paces in front of his crew. He is a tall, well-stacked gent with a scratchy chuckle.

"We heard you peeping over here," he says. "Thought you might be celebrating the day. Thought you might be pleased to step over our way and find out what real celebrating is."

"Thank you, sir," says the Major. "I calculate you're just trying to be neighborly. But we're doing all right ourselves."

"Doing all right?" says the man from Homer's Crossing. "With this ragtag outfit and in this place? Why, I wonder," he says. "I wonder the flag wouldn't be ashamed to be flying around here."

A muttering grumble runs through the crowd of Gulchers. Jim Farrango straightens from a slouch against a tree. That quiet smile begins to play around his lips. Big Joe looms up from a squat on the steps. His big hands begin to curl into big knobby fists.

The man from Horner's Crossing teeters on his boot-soles, rocking from heel to toe and back. His chuckle scratches the air. He is prospecting for tumble-trouble and expects he has found it, and the thought is pleasing to him.

But Jim Farrango slumps against his tree again, the smile fading. Big Joe falls to studying the ground at his feet, letting his hands uncurl loose and limp.

Disappointment shows plain in the man from Horner's Crossing. "Creeping catfish," he says to his crew. "This place beats me. It ain't even got gumption." He stomps off with his crew trailing.

The Gulchers all look at the Major. He is puffing hard and pulling at his chins.

"Well, boys," he says at last, "our parade helped. Sort of put us under the flag, set us down as part of the U.S.A. But we ain't a real town yet."

"Are we licked, Major?" says Storekeeper Murray.

"Certain not," says Pumper Pete. "Name off another thing or two, Major."

"Maybe I can pan out a few more," says the Major. "But they won't assay much. Trouble is the Gulch ain't equipped yet for the things they do in real towns."

"Like what?" says Pumper Pete.

"Like—" says the Major. "Well, like a wedding."

"Hell 'n' Marier," says Pumper Pete. "You got to have a woman for that. One that ain't got a rope on her yet. Reckon we are licked."

"Reckon not," comes a voice from the gathering, piping high with embarrassment but proud too. "Reckon I can take care of that."

Everyone looks at Red Ed Storey. His face is grinning foolish under the rusty beard that scraggles around his chin and up to his ears.

"I got a woman coming to marry me," he says. "Coming on the next stage. A widow lady. Name of Hulda Munson."

Red Ed has never packed much weight in the Gulch before, being a mild man who has arrived late and keeps to himself most of the time. Now he is heavy in the public eye. His shack is rocking every evening with Gulchers offering advice. The Major himself rides all the way to the county seat to be sworn as a justice of the peace so he can perform the ceremony. The Gulch is more excited even than for the parade. The entire tally is determined Red Ed is tied tight and right.

Not a one is missing from the space in front of the Major's emporium when the stage rolls to a stop. Red Ed, uneasy in a starched collar, stands dignified as possible on the steps. Jim Farrango opens the stage door and this woman backs out and to the ground. She turns around. She is short and dumpy with a face like a batch of biscuit dough someone has been working on careless for quite a spell. There is a commotion on the steps and then Red Ed is tearing along the road as fast as he can go.

The woman watches bewildered while Jim Farrango takes her box from the driver and the stage starts off. She picks the Major as the most ample man in view.

"Can you tell me," she says, "where I will find Mr. Storey?"

"Madam," says the Major, bowing as far as his waist will let him, "Madam, that is Mr. Storey hightailing it up the road there."

She stares at the Major and then at the dust whirl that is Red Ed and then she lets a howl and is pounding in the other direction after the stage as fast as plump legs and a hobble skirt will allow. She sees she is losing and stops puffing in the wagon ruts.

She is so golplumed comical standing there, with her hat hanging lopsided over the bun on her head and her shoulders heaving, that chuckles are sprouting into guffaws, when suddenly everyone realizes she is crying. The quick silence is so complete the sobs can be heard clear.

No one seems to know what to do. It is the Major shows what kind of a man he is.

"Jim," he says, "Jim, fetch her into my emporium here. Pete," he says, "you and Big Joe go corral that gallivanting galoot."

Red Ed is still struggling when they bring him in. The shack is full to bulging except for a small space in front of the Major, who has set a chair on a couple of boxes and heaved himself up into it. The woman is at one side of the space, flanked by Mrs. Pumper Pete and Big Joe's squaw. The men hustle Red Ed to the other side facing her. He shudders and pins his eyes to the floor.

"Mr. Storey," says the Major, slow and deliberate, "Mr. Storey, hereinafter to be referred to as Red Ed. Did you or did you not, in the run of epistolary communications with this woman, promise to make her your lawful wedded wife?"

Red Ed scratches busy behind one ear. "I 'fess it straight, Major," he says. "I give my word as per pen and paper right enough. To a woman, yes. But, by cracky, not to this woman."

"No?" says the Major, frowning firm. "Can you stake that? She's shown me the letter."

"Sure can," says Red Ed. He fishes in a hip pocket and hooks out a dog-eared picture card. "I been hiding this so as to surprise you boys. This here is my woman."

The men crowd around and whistles rise free. The woman on the card, smiling sweet under a stylish bonnet, is the kind that any man, howsomever choosy, would be proud to let leave her slippers alongside his bed.

"Hand that here," says the Major. He studies it for a moment. "Red Ed," he says owl solemn, "Red Ed Storey. Are you atrying to josh us?"

"Nary an ounce," says Red Ed. "I'm true talking. That there is my woman. Name of Hulda Munson."

"No," says the Major. "Hulda Munson is this woman standing here. That picture card is the light and glory of the American theeayter. Name of Miss Lillie Langtry."

"Certain is," says Pumper Pete, peering close. "Ed, you been took. Skedaddled up a tree."

"Madam," says the Major, turning to the woman, "we been prepared to use a little persuasion on Red Ed here to behave as a man should when he has spoke pretty to a woman. But it appears you tripped him with crooked dice."

The woman stares steady at the Major, but the blob of dough that is her chin is quivering.

"I never had a picture of my own," she says. "And he's no right to complain. Anyways, I wouldn't marry him iffen he scrooged down in the dirt. Here's what he sent me."

She fumbles in her handbag. She pulls out another picture card. The Major takes it and scowls terrific.

"I'll be broke to the ranks," he says, "if this ain't more of the same. It's the prime player of this whole age. Maurice Barrymore."

"Two of a kind," says Jim Farrango. "A pair of jokers. That's a poor play in any game."

"Maybe not," says the Major. "This is one time two jokers make a pat hand. She tries to fool Red Ed and he tries to fool her, and that stacks it even. Under the circumstances I calculate we can insist they meet the terms agreed and give us our wedding."

"No!" howls Red Ed. "Feed me pizen! But keep her away!"

They can scarce hear him because the woman is wailing her own tune. "No! Not that raggety briar patch. It don't even look like a man."

The Gulchers begin to mutter about feathers and a rail. They have been sighting ahead to a wedding. They take no enjoyment having it scratched. Things are shaping ugly when the Major takes hold again.

"Quiet, boys," he said. "This calls for tactics, Pete," he says, "you and Joe tote Ed here over to your place." He whispers brief in Pumper Pete's ear. "Madam," he says, "you step into my back room. Better do as I say. I'm the law hereabouts. Now the rest of you," he says, "you take care of yourselves outside, for the next hour. Sashay back in here then and we'll proceed with the proceedings."

Punctual on the hour the shack is crowded again. The buzzing is loud, then fades as Pumper Pete and Big Joe show in the doorway. They are pulling a man between them. The other Gulchers look sharp and make out it is Red Ed. The bristles have been shaved away and the top thatch trimmed. There are nicks and red spots around his chin. But he looks younger, plenty cleaner, and almost present-able at a picnic.

The Major comes from the back room, the woman with him. She has shed her hat and her hair is blowing around her head kind of feminine and appealing. The Major climbs to his chair.

"Hulda Munson," he says, "rest your eyes on this man that was hiding behind the whiskers. He ain't one to make the ladies' hearts flutter special fast. But he's a man fair enough. He works reason-able steady. He don't drink more than a man ought. He has a good-paying claim up-creek and he ships dust regular."

The woman looks at Red Ed. You can see she is thinking new thoughts and not shying from them.

"Now," says the Major, waving at her. "Go bring in a piece of that culinary concoction you're keeping warm in my oven." She promenades to the back room. In she come again carrying on a plate a man-size slice of pie.

"Red Ed," says the Major, "take that pie. It's peach. Lucky I had a can for the filling. Eat it. Eat it slow and tasting. She rassled that pie together in a way to bug your eyes."

Red Ed picks the spoon from the plate and tries a bite. He chews it serious and reaches for another. He finishes the whole piece and scrapes for the crust crumbs.

"Red Ed," says the Major, dropping his voice deep, "do you fig-ure you could eat pie like that for the rest of your natural life?"

"I could try," says Red Ed. He flicks his tongue to snag the last crumb from the corner of his mouth. "Yes, by cracky, I could."

"Hulda Munson," says the Major, "do you figure you could stand having this man cluttering your house and caring for your needs the rest of your natural life?"

"Well," she says, coy in her dumpy way, "well, now. If I pushed myself, maybe I might."

"Tactics wins!" shouts Pumper Pete. "Now for our wedding!"

They have their wedding right enough, the best the Major can boss. He decorates the ceremony with all the fancy words he can remember out of years of fancy talking. Storekeeper Murray dusts his fiddle and the men take turns twirling the women till the three of them beg out from worn feet. The toasts are often and hearty, more than sufficient to put a rosy tinge on the lamplight.

They keep it going pretty late. When the whole crowd has walked Red Ed and his new Mrs. home and helped bed them for the night, the regulars reassemble with the Major for a final round.

"Are we a town yet, Major?" says Storekeeper Murray.

The Major is sobering and has his thinking feet under him again.

"I feel better about the Gulch," he says. "A heap better. But I ain't positive." He snaps a finger sudden at Big Joe. "Joe, remember that ornery jumper from the Crossing. If he was here now and blame-talking the Gulch, what would you do?"

Big Joe tries to look fierce. He fails to make it.

"I know how he feels," says Jim Farrango. "Plant the critter here and set him to bragging and I'd be plumb irritated. I'd wish him a deck full of trouble. But I wouldn't feel any compelling call to deal it to him."

The Major wipes a hand across his face. "So we still miss," he says.

"After all that aimin'," says Pumper Pete. "'Taint fair."

"Not fair," says the Major. "But a fact. Must be we been trying to make something you just can't make. I reckon it's got to come natural, sort of grow out of things that happen of themselves."

The regulars meander home, quiet and heavy thinking. They go to bunk feeling mean and crawl out in the morning still tasting the bitter. The Gulch always takes its cue from them and the whole place slows to a dull pace. Three more claims are pegged and a barrel-built man arrives to set up a blacksmith and harness shop and this boosting of the tally hardly helps at all. Not even the news getting about that Mrs. Pumper Pete is expecting to do her share thataway too can whip up much interest.

The Gulch is a glum place these days when a man can walk the full stretch up the creek and never see any but sour faces. Arguments, the slipping into nasty kind, get to be frequent. The days are just days, one tagging another, none standing out special, and they drag past like that until the week of the big rain.

Monday afternoon it starts, a thin drizzle in the Gulch backed by a darkness up in the hills that must mean heavy rain where the thunderheads are hugging the high rocks. Tuesday it is going steady and most of the diggings are too mucky to be worked. By evening the Gulchers notice the creek has crept up a few feet and is throwing an ugly snarl where the current rolls over the shallow spots.

Wednesday morning Storekeeper Murray, whose story-and-a-half hugs the bank, starts moving his stock to the loft as the first trickles creep through his floor boards. Jim Farrango sloshes along and comes in to lend a hand, remarking casual that his shack must be almost to the Missouri by now.

"Rocked me out of bed when she pulled loose," he says. "Just had time to jump clear before she took off. Sailed out of the hollow and headed downstream like Noah's Ark, half under and half showing."

He and Murray with Woolhead Sam helping stow the stuff dry. When they finish, the water is a foot deep around the counters, so they wade out and go upslope to the Major's emporium.

Quite a crowd is collected there. Two other shacks have departed cruising and the talk tells that more will be pulling anchor unless the creek falls mighty soon. The Major is busy chalking his bar for bunk space. The moment he sights Jim and Storekeeper Murray, he begins barking orders.

"Murray," he says, "take a squad here and scurry back to your place. Swim if you have to, but bring me a pile of blankets and a pack of victuals. Jim," he says, "organize a scouting party and work your way upstream. Some of the folks may—"

He stops short, caught by a screech outside coming faint through the drizzle and moving closer. There is a frantic clumping on the steps and Mrs. Red Ed stumbles through the doorway. She looks like a damp dishrag. She has been screeching so long her voice is almost gone, but she is unable to choke it to let real words out. Jim Farrango has to shake her by the shoulders to bring her out of it.

Red Ed, she makes plain at last, is trapped in the tunnel shaft he has driven into the gulch side behind their shack following a good vein into the rock. He has been worried about the rain weakening the side walls and gone in to shore them up and a slide has blocked the entrance. She is sure Red Ed has cashed his chips.

"Nonsense," says the Major. "No rock slide can squelch a Burl's Gulcher, 'specially an ornery maverick as tough as Ed. We'll have him out in a jiffy. Forward, men. On the double."

He is wasting words. The others, Jim Farrango in the lead, are already trooping out the door at a fast trot. The Major is left to do the tagging, which is all a man of his girth can do when hurrying is required. By time he reaches Red Ed's place, puffing noisy but being gallant to the Mrs. by the arm, the rest of the tally is already assembled. They are gathered by the big blob of silt and broken stone that covers the entrance to the tunnel. Pumper Pete is on his knees, scrooging in the dirt with a little pickaxe. The others are standing around watching. Plenty of shovels are in sight, but the men are just leaning on them. The Major plain explodes.

"This ain't a tea party!" he shouts. "Swing those shovels and start digging!"

Pumper Pete looks up. "Major," he says mild, "you don't know a tinker about this kind of work. Stand clear and close your yap." He pivots again to the dirt. In another moment he has uncovered the end of a wooden rail, part of the track Red Ed has been using to bring ore out of the tunnel. He taps it several times with the flat of the pickaxe. He bends to put his ear to the wood. He pulls up and shakes his head and taps again. He bends down. Everyone waits, so quiet only the steady drizzle on the tree leaves can be heard.

Sudden and sharp Pumper Pete jumps up. "Ed's alive!" he says. "Alive and atappin' in there! Hop it, boys. This hill's a bad one an' we'll have to work fast. Three at a time can ditch it to the shaft mouth. The rest of you clear that loose stuff above and drive a row of stakes to hold back any more that has a mind to start movin'."

They fall to, quiet and earnest. The first shift, Big Joe with a pick pacing a pair of husky shovelmen, hits the main digging through the slide.

The Major watches in a moody silence. He tries comforting Mrs. Red Ed and hovering protective by Mrs. Pumper Pete, who ought not be out in such weather in her interesting condition. He shoos them along with Big Joe's squaw into Red Ed's shack and gets them to steaming a wash boiler full of coffee. That kind of piddling doing fails to satisfy. He scours around till he finds a stray shovel and he joins the crew working on the loose slide above the tunnel. He can scarce bend enough to scoop the dirt, but he wheezes game at it.

Pumper Pete sights him fighting the shovel. "Major," he says, "quit that foolishness. You're blocking good diggers."

The Major knows the true when he hears it. He teeters down. "Dogdamn it, Pete," he says, "at a time like now a man's got to do something."

"Certain does," says Pumper Pete. "But no diggin' for you. There's too blame much of you an' all of it gets in the way. Chase on down the line and see how many buckets you can find. Soon as we ditch in deeper we'll have trouble haulin' the stuff out. Too mucky for barrows. A bucket brigade'll do it."

The Major puffs red. "Me!" he says. "You'd make me an errand boy!" He subsides in a slow dwindle. "Yes," he says, "yes. Was I you I'd do the same." He marches off, head up and blinking at the drizzle.

By time he comes back, the upper slide is staked tight. The ditching is close to the shaft mouth, which is uncovered enough to show it is caved part way in.

He can be heard a long ways acoming. He has buckets on ropes bouncing on his back and hanging from his arms and a stack of them upside down on his head. He shakes them in a clatter to the ground in front of Pumper Pete. "Buckets you have," he says. "And I've another little contribution to contribute." He peels his pockets and they pan four bottles of his best rum.

The smell that drifts through the drizzle as the rum joins the coffee in the boiler is enough to make muscles feel big. The mixture itself is positive power in a man. The Gulchers need the lift. They are into the long pull, the period when it's plug along without much progress showing at any particular time and a slump can set in all too easy. Now they settle to the work in a straight earnest, the buckets swinging down the line full from the digging shift and up empty in steady rhythm.

The hours creep past and the morning is gone and the hours creep past and the tunnel is clear maybe a dozen feet in. The opening is twice what it was before from the cave-in, but the rock formation roofing it seems to be holding. All the same, Pumper Pete keeps looking up anxious and bending his head close to the walls like he is listening for whisperings in the rock.

Big Joe is pacing the digging shift again, swinging his pick to loosen the small stuff and using it to pry the big rock chunks. He straightens sudden and lets out a whoop. The point has crashed through to open space beyond. Pumper Pete leaps to the spot. He scraggles a hole with his hands and shouts into it. Faint and a stretch farther a voice answers. The words are muffled in the inner blackness. Pumper Pete listens close. He swings around.

"Ed's pinned by a couple shoring posts," he says. "We'll have to go in and get him. An' fast. The whole hill back there is ready to slip."

He grabs the pick and chokes it short to tear at the hole. He has it about big enough for a man to crawl through when he jumps back, looking up. There is a shivering in the rock. Little cracks fan out from what must be bigger ones farther under out of sight.

He looks quick from one man to another. This is a volunteer job if it is to be done at all. He shakes his shoulders and turns to go himself. He is too late. Jim Farrango is brushing past him.

Jim disappears into the tunnel darkness and before any one of the others thinks to move another man is scrambling after him. It is Woolhead Sam, so frantic in a hurry that he slips back and makes it through the hole only on a second try.

Waiting is a hard doing while the rumbling swells far and deep through the inner rock and the dull sound of chunks falling comes through the hole. Then Jim Farrango's voice is heard, clipped and plain inside.

"We've got him," he is saying. "But he's fainted out cold. Grab aholt."

Red Ed's head and shoulders appear in the hole, limp and bobbing on the dirt. Big Joe hauls him through in one big heave.

The rumbling is becoming a thunder now, and Jim's voice is small over it. "Get going, Sam. Hop into that hole afore I kick you into it."

"No, sir, Jim," they can hear Sam say. "You got to go first. This here rock ain't waitin' for—"

The thunder cuts the rest. Then Jim Farrango's head pops into sight in the hole. He looks surprised and mad and is trying to pull back when Big Joe gets his shoulders and yanks him through.

The thunder is a sustained roar now. The hill seems to shake and settle on itself far inside. The sound drops and dies away in pieces and silence creeps to take and hold the whole world.

It breaks with Jim Farrango cursing soft to himself. "Trumped my ace," he says. "The damned black monkey. Pushed me."

Not much digging is needed this time. They find Sam just beyond the first barrier. He is caught between two big rocks, twisted in a way that tells the full story at once. They carry him to the clear and lay him on the pine needles. His eyes open once and roll till they sight Jim Farrango standing stern to one side. "You all right, Jim?" he says, and his head drops sideways in the last stillness.

They are a wet and dirty crew slogging the mud down creek. Jim Farrango hoists Sam's body to a shoulder and steps off deliberate, and though he has heavy going no one is fool enough to offer help. The Major sends young Mel Osborn ahead to rassle together a blaze in his fireplace. The emporium is beginning to warm when they get there. They crowd in till the entire tally is pressing the walls.

The Major mounts his chair and tunes his vocal cords. He is just getting under way when he stops short. Mrs. Pumper Pete has let out a gasp and clutched Pumper Pete so sudden he has squawked in surprise.

From his high point the Major takes in the situation. "Ladies," he says, "my emporium is at your disposal. The stove, properly coaxed, will heat water as fast as required. Clean flour sacking I use for towels will be found on the shelves." He beams on his brother Gulchers. "There are times," he says, "when words and men are alike useless. This is one."

He shoos them out and follows, dragging Pumper Pete with him. They hunch on the porch and steps, walking careful to avoid Woolhead Sam's body where Jim has laid it out of the wet. The Major pauses by it.

"Might be we'd be rushing things," he says. "But there's no reason we can't give Sam a good funeral right now."

He likes the notion and starts organizing at once and everyone enlists willing. They lay Sam away in a packing case floated from Murray's store. They lower it in a grave dug in the pine grove where Sam liked to smoke a pipe of a lazy evening after chores. They are too busy to notice that the drizzle has dried out of the sky and the afternoon air is brightening clear.

When the case hits bottom, the Major makes to unwind some of his prize oratory. Jim Farrango halts him with a hand on his arm. Jim plants his feet at the grave head.

"Fancy words don't go with Sam," he says. "Might be these will do." He puts his head back and looks up through the tree branches. "There wasn't much of Sam even when he stood tall. But he was man all through. Fate dealt him a mighty poor hand. But he played what cards he had right." Jim reaches in a pocket and brings out a deck. He riffles it and picks out the ace of spades. He steps around the grave and to a pine about twenty paces away and wedges the card in the bark cracks. He steps back to his spot. His hand moves and his gun shows in it and all in almost the same flash five shots shatter the air.

Everyone stares at the card. A jagged hole has blotted the center spade. Jim looks down at the long box. "Sam always did admire my shooting," he says. He reloads the gun slow and silent. He picks up a shovel and starts throwing dirt into the grave. Sunlight comes filtering through the trees and plays on him working there and others join him to give Sam a final covering.

The Major has been still long enough. His voice rolls like a ferry foghorn. "From dust we come. To dust we return. And no man—"

"Shush," says Storekeeper Murray. "Something's doing with the womenfolk."

The Major turns to look at his place off through the trees. Mrs. Red Ed is on the porch waving vigorous. Pumper Pete is leading the stampede in her direction.

The men gather at the foot of the steps, staring up. They wait for Pumper Pete to do the talking. He tries and gulps frantic and tries again, but his throat is cramped tight. Mrs. Red Ed smiles hearty at him. Just as she points inside, they all hear it, a thin and new-sounding wail, kind of astonished and angry at the world, that starts small and grows and then ends in a satisfied gurgle. Pumper Pete makes a terrible effort. "What's the brand?" he says.

Mrs. Red Ed smiles again. "It's a girl," she says. "You can see her soon as we get things ready." She disappears inside.

Pumper Pete's legs are wobbling. He grins foolish and sits down on the steps. The others are joshing him when the delegation arrives.

The man from Homer's Crossing advances ahead of his crew and takes a stand, hands on hips.

"Halloo," he says. "What's the to-doing over here? From the look of things, you're in bad shape. Sort of rained out."

"Rained in," says the Major. "I'd say we're rained in to good shape."

The man from Homer's Crossing stares around at the whole soggy scene. His scratchy chuckle claws along the Gulchers' nerves.

"Why," he says, "you'd shove a man to laugh wasn't he sorry for you. You never had much here worth a brag. Now you've got just about nothing at all."

Big Joe busts out of the crowd of Gulchers. He is moving steady and purposeful and he looms bigger than he ever has before. His eyes are shining and his mouth is twisting and everyone can see that at last he has something to say. He stops, hard on his heels, and works troubled at it and then he has it. "We got a baby," he says.

He moves again, straight for the man from Homer's Crossing. That man grins delighted and waits, rocking on his feet with arms ready. They tangle like a brace of bulls, heaving to throw each other till the sweat streams from them both, then breaking to hammer each other till they have to drag out for breath. Sudden the man drops his head and rams it bitter into Big Joe's midriff, sending him back and down on his buttocks. Immediate the man dives at him, but Big Joe rolls aside and the man lands sprawling. Big Joe is up first and as the man scrambles for footing, Big Joe smashes a fist to the side of his head and puts him down complete.

The Gulchers cheer. The Crossing delegation mutters mad. Hard words are passing when the man pushes to his feet shaking his head to clear the cobwebs.

"Stop the fussing," he tells his crew. "I was spoiling for a fight and this overgrown elk gave it to me. He licked me square and he's the first ever did and I ain't ashamed of it. A tussle like that can knock the grouch out of me for a long spell. It's time we made tracks for home."

He points a friend-like look at Big Joe. "You've got a baby," he says. "Maybe you've even got the makings of a town."

He stomps off, leading his crew, a man who can take a licking and not lose in the taking.

The Gulchers watch him out of sight. "Give him time," says the Major, "and that man will turn out a good neighbor. But he's wrong on that last."

The Major gathers them all in one warm glance. "We've got more than the makings," he says. "I feel it in my marrow the way Big Joe did a few moments ago. Today did it. Life ending and life beginning and all of us pulling together on a tough job. We're a town, boys. Now let's sashay in and have a peck at Miss Pumper Pete."

THE END